Sisters of the Sage

Zane Grey

SISTERS OF THE SAGE

Zane Grey

ALSO BY L.E. MEYER

COMPILATION

The Zane Grey Primer
Zane's Mustangs: An Anthology of Grey's Mustang Stories
Maynard and Zane: Two Icons of the West

FICTION

Canyon Covenants
Double Bit Murder

NON-FICTION

From Sea to Shining Sea
*Zane Grey on Religion (*Transcription with Zen Ervin*)*

COVER DESIGN

Zane Grey Master Character Index
Tales of Florida Fishes
Tales of Oregon Fishes
Riders of the Purple Sage: Arizona Opera Edition
The Rainbow Trail: Arizona Opera Edition

Unidentified Zane Grey friend who looks much like Dolly Grey
L. Tom Perry Collection, BYU, MSS8710, Box 42

SISTERS OF THE SAGE

Zane Grey's
Heroines of the West

Annotated by L.E. Meyer
Introduction by Candace Kant

Zane Grey's West Society

Zane Grey

Credits and permissions for individual stories are listed on
page 327 and are considered a continuation of the this citation.

Sisters of the Sage
Compiled and annotated by Ed Meyer for Zane Grey's West
Society; Introduction by Candace Kant

Library of Congress
Cataloging-in-Publication Data
Zane Grey's West Society
Sisters of the Sage

ISBN: 9781708483678

Cover image: "Jane Withersteen" by William Herbert Dunton,
Riders of the Purple Sage ~ 1912 ~ F & S: serial beginning
Jan 1912

Zane Grey's West Society
www.zgws.org

**DEDICATED TO THE
HEROINES IN OUR LIVES**

WHAT IS WRITING BUT AN EXPRESSION OF MY OWN LIFE?

CONTENTS

Zane and Dolly Grey at their home in Altamont, CA
(L. Tom Perry Collection, BYU, MSS8710, Box 42)

PREFACE

SISTERS OF THE SAGE is a compilation of stories about the greatest heroines in Zane Grey's novels. I accept full responsibility for choosing the courageous women presented in these pages. I hope readers will think about my choices and come to their own conclusions.

Zane Grey labeled himself as an author of Western romances. That's an important distinction. There were great authors of stories about the frontier and the West before Grey. James Fenimore Cooper, Bret Harte and Owen Wister come to mind. Another author we don't hear much about is Clarence E. Mulford. Mulford created Hopalong Cassidy in 1904 and enjoyed a long and successful career with the renowned cowboy hero. You might also include Ned Buntline's dime novels about Buffalo Bill and the westerns by Kurt May over in Germany.

However, with the possible exception of Cooper, heroines were almost an afterthought. Indeed, during most of the 19th century, the term "heroine" in Western literature applied to the love interest of the male protagonist. She was subservient to the hero, not surprising since women in general were subservient in those days. 19th century heroines were not required to display any additional redeeming values.

There were a few notable exceptions who, not surprisingly, were women. Willa Cather's "Pioneer Trilogy" (*O Pioneers!*, *My Antonia!*, and *The Song of the Lark*) are classics with strong heroines as is the entire *Little House on the Prairie* series by Laura Ingalls Wilde. Though her focus was on another frontier (Prince Edward Island, Canada), Lucy Maud Montgomery's *Anne of Green Gables* and its sequels also feature well developed heroines. All three ladies were contemporaries of Zane Grey and perhaps even impacted his perspective of women in literature.

Fortunately, there are several women today who portray women in a light never even imagined by Zane Grey. I personally recommend *The Ordinary Truth* by my friend Jana Richman. She explores the life of three women involved in Nevada's current day struggle by ranchers to preserve their water rights.

In Grey's novels, the ladies were central to every Western romance. The author focused as much on the lovemaking as the adventure itself. While his heroines were typically subservient as well, many women were complex, strong and courageous characters. This decision opened the door to an entirely new audience of young women worldwide making him by far the most published author of his day.

Through the years, critics have panned Zane Grey's writing ability. Personally, I find more recent Western authors like Louis L'Amour, Tony Hillerman, Larry McMurtry, Kent Haruf and Cormac McCarthy to be more accomplished storytellers. However, they wrote for a different audience at a different time and wrote adventure novels, not western romances. Most, if not all, of these authors acknowledged Zane Grey's influence on their work.

One might ask what led to Grey's decision to create a new genre of Westerns. I think there are three primary reasons:

LITERACY IN AMERICA

Zane Grey benefited as public education spread across American in the years preceding his first western romantic fictions, especially among women. Certainly, the market for books and magazine articles skyrocketed across the country as the number of potential readers increased.

After the Civil War, public education became a priority for families across America. One huge contributing factor was the number of illiterate immigrants who came to the United States, largely from Europe during the last half of the 19th century. State and national leaders feared these new citizens would settle in ethnic clusters where they would be slow to adapt the American culture. Consequently, all but six states in the Deep South passed legislation mandating compulsory education for both boys and girls. ("The State of Literacy in America," March 5, 2018)

One-room schoolhouses sprung up in remote communities nationwide. Whereas, early schools were taught by men, unmarried schoolmarms became the norm. Consider this quote from the Littleton School Committee, Littleton, Massachusetts in 1849:

> *God seems to have made woman peculiarly suited to guide and develop the infant mind, and it seems...very poor policy to pay a man 20 or 22 dollars a month, for teaching children the ABCs, when a female could do the work more successfully at one third of the price.*

Young ladies often received even more schooling than their brothers who frequently joined their fathers in the fields when they were of age. Not surprisingly, as America's women became educated, they also became the leaders of both the suffrage and temperance movements. Zane Grey's wife, Dolly, commented on education in the American West while on a 1917 train trip to Glacier National Park and on to the Pacific Coast:

> *We are passing just now through a sort of oasis through which a branch of the Missouri meanders [Dolly was traveling through*

Montana at the time.]. There is fresh green grass, the trees are plentiful and shady and in the prettiest spot, a little new village of small modern houses is springing up. There are even a church and a schoolhouse, white-painted and trim. I notice many schoolhouses through this state and they are all large and fine and seemingly all out of proportion to the few and lovely-looking habitations. I have wondered whether suffrage could have anything to do with this... These states are both enfranchised. At any rate, the same spirit that has given women the vote must have built these attractive schools.

Grey astutely catered both to young men who craved adventure novels and young women who were drawn to his romantic themes.

INSPIRATION FOR GREY'S HEROINES

The topic of who provided the inspiration for Zane Grey's heroes is a sensitive one. I do not want for a second to imply that Zane Grey's actions were always appropriate. My role here is to discuss his heroines, not pass judgement on his behavior.

However, to understand Grey, you need to have background on his plethora of paramours both before and during his marriage. For that reason, Dr. Candace C. Kant has graciously consented to allow her introduction to her groundbreaking work, *Dolly and Zane Grey: Letters from a Marriage*, to also serve as the introduction for *Sisters of the Sage*.

What is important is that these women served as inspiration for many of his heroines along with a few other women like his wife, Dolly, and Louisa Wetherill, wife of the renowned Southwest trader, John Wetherill. Consider this quote from Kant's work:

> *Grey developed deep, involved relationships with each woman that were not just sexual in nature, but emotional and intellectual as well... They aroused in him the emotions that he then channeled into his writing, and they served as the prototypes for his heroines. (Kant, p.6)*

Though Kant's work was a shock to many Grey scholars and viewed with skepticism, her findings were soon reinforced in Thomas H. Pauly's *Zane Grey: His Life, His Adventures, His Women* as well as dozens of letters I read at BYU's *L. Tom Perry Collections* and the *Betty Zane Grosso Collection of Zane and Dolly Grey papers* at Yale University's Beinecke Rare Book and Manuscript Library.

While I will leave it to the reader to pass judgement on the author, if they so choose, I do want to share a personal experience. I wrote two novels in which my characters were composites of my old friends or their ancestors. Whereas I was able to embellish totally fictional characters as I chose, it was not as easy when I dealt with friends and family. No one, for example, wants to be represented as a brutal killer or a prostitute. Consequently, I took special care to present these characters in a more sympathetic manner. Consider how Grey would have developed a heroine, if he had already bragged to a lover that she was the inspiration for the heroine in a novel. Surely, he would have developed a much more complex, courageous character than was the norm in the years leading up to his writing career.

ZANE GREY'S REAL-LIFE HEROINE

In 1905, after five years dating, Zane Grey married Lina Elise Roth (Dolly). When they first met in Lackawaxen, Pennsylvania, Dolly was 17 while Grey was 28. Though Dolly was more than a decade younger than Zane, most researchers acknowledge that she was the glue that kept the Grey family together. In doing so, Dolly was undoubtedly the greatest heroine in the author's life.

In a 1903 letter, Grey recognizes Dolly's importance. "I do put great store in your understanding of me, and your influence over me. Not easy to find a girl to love you. But no one on Earth will find another who can ... make something out of me."

Dolly's motivation in helping Grey, as explained in an early 1905 letter, explains a lot about her personal aspirations:

> *There are times when I myself feel some power stirring in me which seems to drive me to impossible things (for me). It makes me dissatisfied with myself and my surroundings. At such times I wish I were a man, but after a while it usually turns into the channel of wishing to inspire and help you do the great things. What is that feeling---ambition? I think it is higher, more.*

Zane Grey very much needed Dolly's literary skills because his early works were not well received by publishers. *Outing Magazine* provided their perspective on his writing ability when they rejected his *Shores of Lethe*:

> *Sentences as she "called to something submerged deep in him... numb, fearful misery of his face freezing itself in astonishment" is composition run mad. Zane's life, his work was mediocre at best...it is too long, over-drawn in the sense that it leaves little to imagination... it is a muck-raking kind of a story, and I do not believe that the present would be a very good time to go in for any more of that kind of material...I cannot see that it is the kind of thing that would do you and anyone else any good to put on the market in its present state...The best advice to you would be to put it aside for five years, and then take it up again. By that time, you will have acquired a knowledge of the way of putting things that would enable you, I think, to make a good story of it."*

Fortunately, Dolly was herself a gifted writer with a strong educational background in English composition and literature. She pursued a Master's Degree in Education at Columbia College until a serious health issue forced her to temporarily abandon her education. Dolly coached her lover and edited Grey's work for the rest of his life.

Early in his writing career, Zane struggled when writing dialogue. Some critics believe that, when he wrote *Betty Zane*, Dolly may well have shaped how the novel's heroine, Betty was presented. Others think she may have been involved in completing some of Grey's unfinished manuscripts that were sold to Harper Brothers after his death.

So how did Dolly's "touch" impact Grey heroines? Zane's western romance novels were very popular with young women. Many of his stories were first published as serials in *Ladies' Home Journal, McCall's* and *Cosmopolitan.* However, his romances walked on a razor's edge. To a degree, they were the Harlequin romances of the day. Soft sexual innuendo sold, but the Greys had to be careful not to cross the line and drive the ladies away. For this reason, Dolly sometimes reined in Zane's inclination to include salacious passages. Take, for example, this letter to the author about his treatment of Lenore Anderson, the heroine of *The Desert of Wheat*:

> *My God, what hit you when you wrote that chapter? It sounds just as if you'd had a Liebestod session with Mildred Smith (one of Grey's favorite "secretaries). Do you want me to rewrite it?... You've made a beautiful character of Lenore all the way through--- and just here, where she should reach her pinnacle, you've made a nasty little mink out of her.*

It is worth noting that, during the years before and after the start of the 20th century, women were asserting themselves, less satisfied with simply sitting back and being the subservient helpmate of their men. They longed for tales of bold women willing to step forward and contribute to their own fate. Not surprisingly, Dolly was a suffragette and likely to push back when Zane created a shallow heroine.

In *Sisters of the Sage* you will find stories of strong, intelligent women. Included with each story is a brief discussion of the kind of courage shown by the story's heroine. You will learn that heroism does not always involve sic-shooter and physical courage. I hope these tales resonate with the world in which you live today.

Ed Meyer
Editor

Editor's Note: I shared many historic photos in *Sisters of the Sage*. Most were taken between 1910 and 1925, typically by Zane Grey himself. The originals are generally beautiful, especially given their age. However, several images "blurred" a bit during the production of the book. I chose to include them anyway for your enjoyment and their historic importance.

Ed Meyer is the marketing director of Zane Grey's West Society. He contributes articles regularly to the Society's publication, the Zane Grey Explorer and creates collections of Grey's works tailored to readers new to the author's writings. In addition to Sisters of the Sage, these collections include The Zane Grey Primer and Zane's Mustangs. He is also a contributor to Tales of Florida Fishes. Meyer also penned a historic fiction novel about James Simpson Emett, the man Grey said influenced him most, entitled Canyon Covenants.

Meyer received an undergraduate degree in anthropology from the University of Utah and a master's degree in public administration from Brigham Young University. He is retired living in Florence, Arizona with his wife, Kathy.

Zane Grey

Sisters of the Sage

ACKNOWLEDGMENTS

SISTERS OF THE SAGE was an unexpected adventure for me. I was doing just fine until my wife, Kathy, asked if I had run the book past any women, given I was a man. Gulp, so I did! Thanks to all the women who shared their very diverse perspectives with me.

Special thanks go to four women who spent significant time critiquing the book. These include Bonnie Pratt, Rosanne Vrugtman, Jan Gautreaux and my wife, Kathy. I also thank Jan for applying her considerable proofreading and formatting skills to *Sisters of the Sage*.

I acknowledge the generosity of Dr. Candace Kant for granting her permission to use her introduction from *Dolly and Zane Grey: Letters from a Marriage* and Harvey Leake for letting us include his story about his great-grandmother, Louisa Wetherill, "Slim Woman of Kayenta."

Finally, thanks go to the L. Tom Perry Collections at Brigham Young University, Zane Grey's West Society and the John and Louisa Wetherill Collection for the images that add so much to the book.

Ed Meyer

Sisters of the Sage

Dolly & Zane Grey

LETTERS FROM A MARRIAGE

Edited and with commentary by CANDACE C. KANT

INTRODUCTION

CANDACE KANT is generously contributing the introduction from her work, Zane and Dolly Grey: Letters from a Marriage, *for use as the introduction to* Sisters of the Sage *as well.*

While Grey is commended for the heroines in his works, in the interests of full disclosure, the reader should understand the Grey's unique lifestyle. The intent is not to condemn or condone the choices they made. It was a different time that is hard to measure by today's standards. However, a greater comprehension of the Greys may help the reader relate to the heroines in the stories.

IT IS IMPOSSIBLE to estimate the impact Zane Grey had on the reading and movie-viewing public in the early years of the twentieth century without resorting to anecdote. His first successful novel, *Heritage of the Desert* (1910), sold over eight hundred thousand copies. His second, *Riders of the Purple Sage* (1912), sold over one million copies in its first year of publication, making Zane Grey an author of national and even international reputation. His literary output was overwhelming by any measure.

By his death in 1939, his writing filled over ninety-six volumes, including western romances, short stories, baseball tales, fishing adventure sagas, one novel set in Tahiti, and another set in Australia. His books were on bestseller lists in hardbound editions beginning in 1913 with *The Lone Star Ranger*, again in 1917 with *Wildfire*, and then every year thereafter from 1917 to 1924. Zane Grey became the name for a huge enterprise based on his writing, including magazine serials, hardbound books, international editions, movie versions, stage versions, children's books and, eventually, a corporate structure. The public demand for his work was immeasurable. His wife Dolly once wrote, "You, the man, must live up to the name you have created. You can't quit. You can't be anything but great. You dare not. In that sense, you don't even belong to yourself, but to the millions to whom you stand for an ideal."

As usual she was right, at least in part, for he had not created that name alone. Dolly Grey guided, directed, and managed Zane Grey's career just as surely as if she were his business partner rather than his wife. Her role has been neglected by others who examined his life, because it was not a public role. He supplied the imagination, the ability to transform the emotions he felt into the western romance he wrote, and the name. She supplied the expertise in editing and the business acumen, for she managed all affairs with editors, publishers, and Hollywood producers and directors.

Together they created an image that defined their outward lives. Grey's books were promoted as reading material appropriate for all ages, from young readers to the aged, acceptable both in schools and in libraries. Should there be anything in his personal life that contradicted this image, the marketability of his work would suffer. And there was something in his personal life that threatened his success: his numerous affairs with other women.

In two senses Grey's life was itself a fiction. Outwards, he lived a conventional married life with Dolly and their three children. But this was a façade that concealed his many dalliances with young women, which both Zane and Dolly took great pains to hide. Ironically, this hidden life also contained elements of fantasy. In it he lived and relived the romantic plots he created casting himself as the romantic hero, wooing and winning the young and beautiful heroine. In a letter to Robert Herbert Davis, Zane's friend and literary agent, Dolly referred in an oblique way to this trait, writing "the man has always lived in a land of make-believe, and has clothed all of his own affairs in the shining garments of romance, and it is as if these were rent and torn and smirched." While she was referring to Zane's reaction to John O'Hara's

Appointment of Samarra, her words speak volumes about Zane's mind.

Much of Zane and Dolly's married life was spent apart. In the early years, he traveled in the West three to four months out of the year then spent the coldest months of the winter in Long Key, Florida, or in California, usually with feminine companions, leaving Dolly behind. Later, in the twenties, he discovered the South Seas and fished there for as much as six months at a time, spending more time in Oregon in the summers. The two maintained their relationship through letters, thousands of letters, written over a span of thirty-nine years, from the time they met in 1900 until his death in 1939. These letters run the gamut of emotions from mushy love letters to bitter documents full of animosity, from reports of business matters to reproaches regarding failures and mistakes.

The letters reveal that their marriage was anything but ordinary. Indeed, throughout the thirty-four-year marriage Dolly was far from the only woman in Zane's life. What is even more startling is that she was completely aware of it and, in order to conceal the truth from the public, became an unwilling accomplice. She knew of this part of his nature from the years of their courtship and at least initially hoped that he would leave this behind him as marriage provided for his emotional and physical needs. That was not to be, and Dolly had to adjust to the reality of what her relationship to her husband was. She endured years of bitter loneliness, and for a time the marriage was in great peril, but divorce was unthinkable to women of her class and station in that time period, particularly those with children. In 1911 she wrote in her diary, "Marriage is for children. They are the closest bond between husband and wife, a bond which should hold when all other things fail."

After the move to California in 1918, she emerged from her ordeal with resignation to his habits and determination to be everything else to her husband, if not his only lover. She came to look upon her earlier self as a "fearful prude" and wrote in her diary that it was "only the California atmosphere, or perhaps I should say the western environment, that finally released me after the age of thirty." Not only did she accept his habits, she collaborated in hiding them from the public, actively protecting him from the consequences of his actions, which often were naïve, thoughtless, and irresponsible. The women were referred to as secretaries (who did little typing), nieces (of which he had none), or literary assistants (who he did not need, since he had Dolly). Chaperones were along to prevent talk, and Dolly even hosted the women in her own home, her presence assuring the appearance of propriety. Instead of dwelling on the failings of her marriage, she concentrated on building a financial empire based on his work.

Money earned from his writing was divided in half. He used his portion for yachts and fishing. She put hers in real-estate and stock-market investments, eventually becoming the president of a bank.

In the relaxed atmosphere of Southern California, with the presence of the film industry and the increasing availability and acceptance of divorce in the twenties, Dolly still did not leave her philandering husband. This might be attributed to her affinity for his great wealth, but according to the divorces granted in those days, she would have received a large portion of the wealth earned and rights to that yet to be earned, so that reason does not stand the test. It might be said that she had become accustomed to the lifestyle, with a house in Catalina and another in Altadena, servants, luxury, cars, and the respect and privilege afforded to her as Mrs. Zane Grey. But her letters suggest that all that meant only additional worries for her. What does stand out is her unwavering belief in his genius, steadfast commitment to him, understanding of the demons that plagued him, and a genuine affection. On their twenty-ninth anniversary she wrote,

> *I wonder if anyone has had as varied and eventful a life as I have during twenty-nine-years. After all, despite the fact that I dare not mention all this passage of time to Z.G., I think it is quite an achievement*

> *to be "Happy Through Marriage" for*
> *such a long time. But it has always been*
> *my claim that friendship and*
> *understanding and a working together are*
> *the basis for lasting marriages. I will not*
> *say that the modern method of on again off*
> *again may not be better. Perhaps I should*
> *not compare them at all. Perhaps what*
> *they do now with short marriages and*
> *easy divorces are a product of the times*
> *and a necessity of the times. However,*
> *even the people of our generation are*
> *getting their divorces just the same. But*
> *somehow, I have the feeling that Doc and*
> *I will stick it out to the end, even though I*
> *would never seek to hold him if he desired*
> *any other arrangement.*

The portrait of Zane that emerges from his letters is not always a flattering one, and his fans may well be dismayed. It should be remembered, however, that he was a product of his times, and in that era the peccadillos of men, particularly wealthy men, were winked at by society. Indeed, Dolly looked realistically at the environment into which Zane had been born, and she once remarked about his family that "they have always believed that man can do anything, but that a woman should be above reproach." Zane could hardly have helped having this point of view himself.

In the early years of his marriage, Zane earnestly tried not to give in to temptation, but he usually failed. In a letter written in 1906, shortly after his marriage, he tells Dolly of his struggles,

I have tried to stop profanity. The old words fly to my lips. I have tried to kill the deadly sweetness of conscious power over women. A pair of dark blue eyes makes me a tiger. I loved my sweetheart in honest ways more than any other. I love my wife, yet such iron I am that there is no change.

He tried to hide his dalliances from her, but she always knew.

When money began pouring in after the publication of *Heritage of the Desert* in 1910 and he was able to indulge his desires, he made no further attempt to shield her from his nature, doing exactly what he wanted, at a cost to all those around him. Nevertheless, it would be an error to conclude that he was heartless. He sincerely loved his wife and deeply regretted causing her pain, but he equally sincerely felt that the emotions aroused in him by his flirtations were necessary to his writing and were poured into his work. Holding her to a higher standard than he set for himself, he believed her jealousy was a base emotion that she should be able to rise above, seeing his true nature. And with a twisted perspective of reality, he denied any immorality. Writing to his friend Alvah Jones, he said,

> *When I read some of your letter to Dolly, she asked, "What does he mean by moral?" So far as I am concerned, I can remember only a couple or at most very few times when I might have been called immoral. And even then, considering my simplicity, my intensity, my sincerity, I doubt that it could have been called so. Every emotion I ever had has gone into my books.*

When he was honest with himself, which happened most often in the midst of one of his black moods or when he awoke in the middle of the night, he bitterly reproached himself for his failings, particularly for having hurt Dolly. This happened more often as he grew older. Writing to James in 1936, he stated, "No doubt you sacrificed yourself for your family. I never did that, I sacrificed everybody." Self-doubt and periodic bouts of depression, which he called his black moods, tortured him. For all his pursuits- fishing, baseball, women, writing- the prize always eluded him. Never trusting those around him, convinced that he was surrounded by conspiracies, he never allowed anyone except Dolly to be truly emotionally close to him. Perhaps that was a result of the hidden portion of his life, which made him suspicious and untrusting. Although surrounded by an entourage at all times, he was always lonely. In all of the letters over thirty-nine years, he only once stated that he felt really happy.

As to the exact nature of his relationships with the other women, it is impossible to say. Ambiguity will always remain, because the letters written to them and by them were destroyed after his death. Those few letters that exist do not deal with any matters of substance or emotion. We have only what Dolly and Zane said in regards to those relationships in their letters to each other. Yet that is enough to conclude that these affairs were both emotional and physical and were sufficiently threatening that both Zane and Dolly made every attempt to cloak them with a respectability they did not have.

Grey developed deep, involved relationships with each woman that were not just sexual in nature, but emotional and intellectual as well. He remained involved with the women for long periods of time, in Mildred Smith's case for over fifteen years. And for Zane the women were part of his work, or so he thought. They aroused in him the emotions that he then channeled into his writing, and they served as prototypes for his heroines, sometimes directly, like Lillian Wilhelm for Mescal in *Heritage of the Desert* and Bernice

Campbell for Martha Ann Dixon in *Wyoming*, for example, but more frequently, as composites of the women he had known. Dolly once wrote with great insight, "A genius needs to be fed by many personalities which he mashes and grinds up as a mill does, in order to get the finished product."

Dolly was talented, capable, well educated in her own right, and ambitious, but she was willing to play a secondary, supportive role. She has appeared superhumanly tolerant, patient, and long suffering, sacrificing her immediate needs for a larger vision. In reality she has been defined by men, reduced to the supporting role while Zane has been the star. Now her voice, clear and articulate, reveals that she was not the long-suffering, self-sacrificing victim, although she did like to paint herself that way to her husband. She had a voice and a will of her own. She was accomplished, confident, comfortable with publishers, movie-studio heads, and bank presidents. She was the one solid, steadying influence for her children and her famous husband. She was his Northern Star. They completed each other. Zane Grey would never have been the success he was if there had been no Dolly.

Candace C. Kant
From *Dolly and Zane Grey:*
Letters from a Marriage

CANDACE KANT holds a bachelor's degree in U.S. history and Master's Degree in U.S Colonial Social and Intellectual History from the University of Nevada and earned a Ph.D. in history from Northern Arizona University. Her Zane Grey's Arizona *won the Southwest Border Library award.* She also wrote Dolly and Zane Grey: Letters from a Marriage. *She was awarded the title Emerita in 2008 after teaching history, women's study and religious study courses at the College of Southern Nevada for 32 years.*

CHAPTER 1

BETTY ZANE

From *Betty Zane* (1903)

BETTY ZANE was the first of Zane Grey's
Ohio River Trilogy, a three-book series about his
frontier ancestors, the Zanes. These hardy pioneers
lived on the Ohio River in Fort Henry, near present
day Wheeling, West Virginia.

Some researchers believe Grey's wife, Dolly
played a role in developing the title character,
Betty, in Grey's first novel, **Betty Zane**. Certainly,
Betty and Dolly shared a few similar thoughts
about men. Thomas Pauly writes, "She [Betty]
notices that men enjoy greater privilege, and she
resents it. She complains at one point, 'It is always
a man that spoils everything... I envy your being a
man... You have a world to conquer. A woman,
what can she do?" (Pauly 49) Dolly Grey shared
similar feelings at times with her husband.

The story shared here retells an actual historic
event. British and Indian forces are attacking the
settlers at Fort Henry. Defenders in the fort walls
run out of gunpowder and will surely die if they do
not receive more powder from a nearby cabin.
Young Betty Zane saves the day through an exciting
"race with death."

There are lots of characters in the story so a quick introduction of a few of them is in order. All of the men with the surname Zane are brothers defending the fort and the cabin. Their sister is Betty. Her lover is Alfred Clarke. Lewis Wetzel is a famous Indian fighter.

Betty is a classic heroine who physically risks her life to save others. As we will see, other Zane Grey heroines often display their bravery in other ways that are equally meritorious.

THE SUN ROSE RED. Its ruddy rays peeped over the eastern hills, kissed the tree-tops, glinted along the stony bluffs, and chased away the gloom of night from the valley. Its warm gleams penetrated the portholes of the Fort and cast long bright shadows on the walls; but it brought little cheer to the sleepless and almost exhausted defenders. It brought to many of the settlers the familiar old sailor's maxim: "Red sky at morning, sailor's warning." Rising in its crimson glory the sun flooded the valley, dyeing the river, the leaves, the grass, the stones, tinging everything with that awful color which stained the stairs, the benches, the floor, even the portholes of the block-house.

Historians call this the time that tried men's souls. If it tried the men, think what it must have been to those grand, heroic women. Though they had helped the men load and fire nearly forty-eight hours; though they had worked without a moment's rest and were now ready to succumb to exhaustion; though the long room was full of stifling smoke and the sickening odor of burned wood and powder, and though the row of silent, covered bodies had steadily lengthened, the thought of giving up never occurred to the women. Death there would be sweet compared to what it would be at the hands of the redmen.

At sunrise Silas Zane, bare-chested, his face dark and fierce, strode into the bastion which was connected with the blockhouse. It was a small shed-like room with portholes opening to the river and the forest. This bastion had seen the severest fighting.

Five men had been killed here. As Silas entered, four haggard and powder-begrimed men kneeling before the portholes, looked up at him. A dead man lay in one corner.

"Smith's dead. That makes fifteen," said Silas. "Fifteen out of forty-two, that leaves twenty-seven. We must hold out. Len, don't expose yourselves recklessly. How goes it at the south bastion?"

"All right. There's been firin' over there all night," answered one of the men. "I guess it's been kinder warm over that way. But I ain't heard any shootin' for some time."

"Young Bennet is over there, and if the men needed anything, they would send him for it," answered Silas. "I'll send some food and water. Anything else?"

"Powder. We're nigh out of powder," replied the man addressed. "And we might jes as well make ready fer a high old time. The red devils hadn't been quiet all this last hour fer nothin'."

Silas passed along the narrow hallway which led from the bastion into the main room of the block-house. As he turned the corner at the head of the stairway, he encountered a boy who was dragging himself up the steps.

"Hello! Who's this? Why, Harry!" exclaimed Silas, grasping the boy and drawing him into the room. Once in the light Silas saw that the lad was so weak, he could hardly stand. He was covered with blood. It dripped from a bandage wound tightly about his arm; it oozed through a hole in his hunting shirt, and it flowed from a wound over his temple. The shadow of death was already stealing over the pallid face, but from the grey eyes shone an indomitable spirit, a spirit which nothing but death could quench.

"Quick!" the lad panted. "Send men to the south wall. The redskins are breakin' in where the water from the spring runs under the fence."

"Where are Metzar and the other men?"

"Dead! Killed last night. I've been there alone all night. I kept on shootin'. Then I gets plugged here under the chin. Knowin' it's all up with me I deserted my post when I heard the Injuns choppin' on the fence where it was on fire last night. But I only—run—because—they're gettin' in."

"Wetzel, Bennet, Clarke!" yelled Silas, as he laid the boy on the bench.

Almost as Silas spoke the tall form of the hunter confronted him.

Clarke and the other men were almost as prompt.

"Wetzel, run to the south wall. The Indians are cutting a hole through the fence."

Wetzel turned, grabbed his rifle and an axe and was gone like a flash.

"Sullivan, you handle the men here. Bessie, do what you can for this brave lad. Come, Bennet, Clarke, we must follow Wetzel," commanded Silas.

Mrs. Zane hastened to the side of the fainting lad. She washed away the blood from the wound over his temple. She saw that a bullet had glanced on the bone and that the wound was not deep or dangerous. She unlaced the hunting shirt at the neck and pulled the flaps apart. There on the right breast, on a line with the apex of the lung, was a horrible gaping wound. A murderous British slug had passed through the lad. From the hole at every heart-beat poured the dark, crimson life-tide. Mrs. Zane turned her white face away for a second; then she folded a small piece of linen, pressed it tightly over the wound, and wrapped a towel round the lad's breast.

"Don't waste time on me. It's all over," he whispered. "Will you call Betty here a minute?"

Betty came, white-faced and horror-stricken. For forty hours she had been living in a maze of terror. Her movements had almost become mechanical. She had almost ceased to hear and feel. But the light in the eyes of this dying boy brought her back to the horrible reality of the present.

"Oh, Harry! Harry! Harry!" was all Betty could whisper.

"I'm goin', Betty. And I wanted—you to say a little prayer for me—and say good-bye to me," he panted.

Betty knelt by the bench and tried to pray.

"I hated to run, Betty, but I waited and waited and nobody came, and the Injuns was gettin' in. They'll find dead Injuns in piles out there. I was shootin' fer you, Betty, and every time I aimed I thought of you."

The lad rambled on, his voice growing weaker and weaker and finally ceasing. The hand which had clasped Betty's so closely loosened its hold. His eyes closed. Betty thought he was dead, but no! he still breathed. Suddenly his eyes opened. The shadow of pain was gone. In its place shone a beautiful radiance.

"Betty, I've cared a lot for you—and I'm dyin'—happy because I've fought fer you—and somethin' tells me—you'll—be saved. Good-bye." A smile transformed his face and his gray eyes gazed steadily into hers. Then his head fell back. With a sigh his brave spirit fled.

Wetzel joined them at this moment, and they hurried back to the block-house. The firing had ceased on the bluff. They met Sullivan at the steps of the Fort. He was evidently coming in search of them.

"Zane, the Indians and the Britishers are getting ready for more determined and persistent effort than any that has yet been made," said Sullivan.

"How so?" asked Silas.

"They have got hammers from the blacksmith's shop, and they boarded my boat and found a keg of nails. Now they are making a number of ladders. If they make a rush all at once and place ladders against the fence, we'll have the Fort full of Indians in ten minutes. They can't stand in the face of a cannon charge. We must use the cannon."

"Clarke, go into Capt. Boggs' cabin and fetch out two kegs of powder," said Silas.

The young man turned in the direction of the cabin, while Silas and the others ascended the stairs.

"The firing seems to be all on the south side," said Silas, "and is not so heavy as it was."

"Yes, as I said, the Indians on the river front are busy with their new plans," answered Sullivan.

"Why does not Clarke return?" said Silas, after waiting a few moments at the door of the long room. "We have no time to lose. I want to divide one keg of that powder among the men."

Clarke appeared at the moment. He was breathing heavily as though he had run up the stairs, or was laboring under a powerful emotion. His face was gray.

"I could not find any powder!" he exclaimed. "I searched every nook and corner in Capt. Boggs' house. There is no powder there."

A brief silence ensued. Everyone in the block-house heard the young man's voice. No one moved.

They all seemed waiting for someone to speak. Finally, Silas Zane burst out:

"Not find it? You surely could not have looked well. Capt. Boggs himself told me there were three kegs of powder in the storeroom. I will go and find it myself."

Alfred did not answer, but sat down on a bench with an odd numb feeling round his heart. He knew what was coming. He had been in the Captain's house and had seen those kegs of powder. He knew exactly where they had been. Now they were not on the accustomed shelf, nor at any other place in the storeroom. While he sat there waiting for the awful truth to dawn on the garrison, his eyes roved from one end of the room to the other. At last they found what they were seeking. A young woman knelt before a charcoal fire which she was blowing with a bellows. It was Betty. Her face was pale and weary, her hair disheveled, her shapely arms blackened with charcoal, but notwithstanding she looked calm, resolute, self-contained. Lydia was kneeling by her side holding a bullet-mold on a block of wood. Betty lifted the ladle from the red coals and poured the hot metal with a steady hand and an admirable precision. Too much or too little lead would make an imperfect ball. The little missile had to be just so for those soft-metal, smooth-bore rifles. Then Lydia dipped the mold in a bucket of water, removed it and knocked it on the floor. A small, shiny lead bullet rolled out. She rubbed it with a greasy rag and then dropped it in a jar. For nearly forty hours, without sleep or rest, almost without food, those brave girls had been at their post.

Silas Zane came running into the room. His face was ghastly, even his lips were white and drawn.

"Sullivan, in God's name, what can we do? The powder is gone!" he cried in a strident voice.

"Gone?" repeated several voices.

"Gone?" echoed Sullivan. "Where?"

"God knows. I found where the kegs stood a few days ago. There were marks in the dust. They have been moved."

"Perhaps Boggs put them here somewhere," said Sullivan. "We will look."

"No use. No use. We were always careful to keep the powder out of here on account of fire. The kegs are gone, gone."

"Miller stole them," said Wetzel in his calm voice.

"What difference does that make now?" burst out Silas, turning passionately on the hunter, whose quiet voice in that moment seemed so unfeeling. "They're gone!"

In the silence which ensued after these words the men looked at each other with slowly whitening faces. There was no need of words. Their eyes told one another what was coming. The fate which had overtaken so many border forts was to be theirs.

They were lost! And every man thought not of himself, cared not for himself, but for those innocent children, those brave young girls and heroic women.

A man can die. He is glorious when he calmly accepts death; but when he fights like a tiger, when he stands at bay his back to the wall, a broken weapon in his hand, bloody, defiant, game to the end, then he is sublime. Then he wrings respect from the souls of even his bitterest foes. Then he is avenged even in his death.

But what can women do in times of war? They help, they cheer, they inspire, and if their cause is lost, they must accept death or worse. Few women have the courage for self-destruction. "To the victor belong the spoils," and women have ever been the spoils of war.

No wonder Silas Zane and his men weakened in that moment. With only a few charges for their rifles and none for the cannon how could they hope to hold out against the savages? Alone they could have drawn their tomahawks and have made a dash through the lines of Indians, but with the women and the children that was impossible.

"Wetzel, what can we do? For God's sake, advise us!" said Silas hoarsely. "We cannot hold the Fort without powder. We cannot leave the women here. We had better tomahawk every woman in the block-house than let her fall into the hands of Girty."

"Send someone fer powder," answered Wetzel.

"Do you think it possible," said Silas quickly, a ray of hope lighting up his haggard features. "There's plenty of powder in Eb's cabin. Whom shall we send? Who will volunteer?"

Three men stepped forward, and others made a movement.

"They'd plug a man full of lead afore he'd get ten foot from the gate," said Wetzel. "I'd go myself, but it wouldn't do no good. Send a boy, and one as can run like a streak."

"There are no lads big enough to carry a keg of powder. Harry Bennett might go," said Silas. "How is he, Bessie?"

"He is dead," answered Mrs. Zane.

Wetzel made a motion with his hands and turned away. A short, intense silence followed this indication of hopelessness from him. The women understood, for some of them covered their faces, while others sobbed.

"I will go."

It was Betty's voice, and it rang clear and vibrant throughout the room. The miserable women raised their drooping heads, thrilled by that fresh young voice. The men looked stupefied. Clarke seemed turned to stone. Wetzel came quickly toward her.

"Impossible!" said Sullivan.

Silas Zane shook his head as if the idea were absurd.

"Let me go, brother, let me go?" pleaded Betty as she placed her little hands softly, caressingly on her brother's bare arm. "I know it is only a forlorn chance, but still it is a chance. Let me take it. I would rather die that way than remain here and wait for death."

"Silas, it ain't a bad plan," broke in Wetzel. "Betty can run like a deer. And bein' a woman they may let her get to the cabin without shootin'."

Silas stood with arms folded across his broad chest. As he gazed at his sister great tears coursed down his dark cheeks and splashed on the hands which so tenderly clasped his own. Betty stood before him transformed; all signs of weariness had vanished; her eyes shone with a fateful resolve; her white and eager face was surpassingly beautiful with its light of hope, of prayer, of heroism.

"Let me go, brother. You know I can run, and oh! I will fly today. Every moment is precious. Who knows? Perhaps Capt. Boggs is already near at hand with help. You cannot spare a man. Let me go."

"Betty, Heaven bless and save you, you shall go," said Silas.

"No! No! Do not let her go!" cried Clarke, throwing himself before them. He was trembling, his eyes were wild, and he had the appearance of a man suddenly gone mad.

"She shall not go," he cried.

"What authority have you here?" demanded Silas Zane, sternly. "What right have you to speak?"

"None, unless it is that I love her and I will go for her," answered Alfred desperately.

"Stand back!" cried Wetzel, placing his powerful hard on Clarke's breast and pushing him backward. "If you love her you don't want to have her wait here for them red devils," and he waved his hand toward the river. "If she gets back, she'll save the Fort. If she fails, she'll at least escape Girty."

Betty gazed into the hunter's eyes and then into Alfred's. She understood both men. One was sending her out to her death because he knew it would be a thousand times more merciful than the fate which awaited her at the hands of the Indians. The other had not the strength to watch her go to her death. He had offered himself rather than see her take such fearful chances.

"I know. If it were possible you would both save me," said Betty, simply. "Now you can do nothing but pray that God may spare my life long enough to reach the gate. Silas, I am ready."

Downstairs a little group of white-faced men were standing before the gateway. Silas Zane had withdrawn the iron bar. Sullivan stood ready to swing in the ponderous gate. Wetzel was speaking with a clearness and a rapidity which were wonderful under the circumstances.

"When we let you out, you'll have a clear path. Run, but not very fast. Save your speed. Tell the Colonel to empty a keg of powder in a table cloth. Throw it over your shoulder and start back. Run like you was racin' with me, and keep on comin' if you do get hit. Now go!"

The huge gate creaked and swung in. Betty ran out, looking straight before her. She had covered half the distance between the Fort and the Colonel's house when long taunting yells filled the air.

"Squaw! Waugh! Squaw! Waugh!" yelled the Indians in contempt.

Not a shot did they fire. The yells ran all along the river front, showing that hundreds of Indians had seen the slight figure running up the gentle slope toward the cabin.

Betty obeyed Wetzel's instructions to the letter. She ran easily and not at all hurriedly, and was as cool as if there had not been an Indian within miles.

Col. Zane had seen the gate open and Betty come forth. When she bounded up the steps, he flung open that door and she ran into his arms.

"Betts, for God's sake! What's this?" he cried.

"We are out of powder. Empty a keg of powder into a table cloth. Quick! I've not a second to lose," she answered, at the same time slipping off her outer skirt. She wanted nothing to hinder that run for the block-house.

Jonathan Zane heard Betty's first words and disappeared into the magazine-room. He came out with a keg in his arms. With one blow of an axe he smashed in the top of the keg. In a twinkling a long black stream of the precious stuff was piling up in a little hill in the center of the table. Then the corners of the table cloth were caught up, turned and twisted, and the bag of powder was thrown over Betty's shoulder.

"Brave girl, so help me God, you are going to do it!" cried Col. Zane, throwing open the door. "I know you can. Run as you never ran in all your life."

Like an arrow sprung from a bow Betty flashed past the Colonel and out on the green. Scarcely ten of the long hundred yards had been covered by her flying feet when a roar of angry shouts and yells warned Betty that the keen-eyed savages saw the bag of powder and now knew they had been deceived by a girl. The cracking of rifles began at a point on the bluff nearest Col. Zane's house, and extended in a half circle to the eastern end of the clearing. The leaden messengers of Death whistled past Betty. They sped before her and behind her, scattering pebbles in her path, striking up the dust, and ploughing little furrows in the ground. A quarter of the distance covered! Betty had passed the top of the knoll now and she was going down the gentle slope like the wind. None but a fine marksman could have hit that small, flitting figure. The yelling and screeching had become deafening. The reports of the rifles blended in a roar. Yet above it all Betty heard Wetzel's stentorian yell. It lent wings to her feet. Half the distance covered! A hot, stinging pain shot through Betty's arm, but she heeded it not. The bullets were raining about her. They sang over her head; hissed close to her ears, and cut the grass in front of her; they pattered like hail on the stockade-fence, but still untouched, unharmed, the slender brown figure sped toward the gate. Three-fourths of the distance covered! A tug at the flying hair, and a long, black tress cut off by a bullet, floated away on the breeze. Betty saw the big gate swing; she saw the tall figure of the hunter; she saw her brother. Only a few more yards! On! On! On! A blinding red mist obscured her sight. She lost the opening in the fence, but unheeding she rushed on. Another second and she stumbled; she felt herself grasped by eager arms; she heard the gate slam and the iron bar shoot into place; then she felt and heard no more.

Silas Zane bounded up the stairs with a doubly precious burden in his arms. A mighty cheer greeted his entrance. It aroused Alfred Clarke, who had bowed his head on the bench and had lost all sense of time and place. What were the women sobbing and crying over? To whom belonged that white face? Of course, it was the face of the girl he loved. The face of the girl who had gone to her death. And he writhed in his agony.

Then something wonderful happened. A warm, living flush swept over that pale face. The eyelids fluttered; they opened, and the dark eyes, radiant, beautiful, gazed straight into Alfred's.

Still Alfred could not believe his eyes. That pale face and the wonderful eyes belonged to the ghost of his sweetheart. They had come back to haunt him. Then he heard a voice.

"O-h! but that brown place burns!"

Alfred saw a bare and shapely arm. Its beauty was marred by a cruel red welt. He heard that same sweet voice laugh and cry together. Then he came back to life and hope. With one bound he sprang to a porthole.

"God, what a woman!" he said between his teeth, as he thrust the rifle forward.

CHAPTER 2

LUCINDA HUETT

From *30,000 on the Hoof* (1940)

ZANE GREY'S NOVEL, 30,000 on the Hoof, *spans three generations of a frontier cattle ranching family. Logan Huett brings his bride, Lucinda, to a remote Arizona valley which they homestead for three decades. Together they overcome harsh weather, marauding bands of Indians and rustlers. The hardy couple raises three boys and adopts a girl abandoned on the trail. The youngest boy, Abe, marries the girl, Barb, and soon there's a grandchild in the Huett family. With the pending sale of a huge herd of cattle, Logan and Lucinda move to "Flag" where they can enjoy their golden years in the comfort of city life. Then tragedy strikes. Logan loses his cattle to dishonest cattle buyers and news comes that two of their sons have died in World War I while the third son, Abe, is missing in action. The two disasters overwhelm both Logan and their adopted daughter, Barbara. Their spirit to survive is lost.*

In this touching story, Lucinda is a much different heroine from Betty Zane. While Betty's courage is obvious as she physically defies danger, Lucinda shows MORAL courage as she rescues her family from the depths of depression and despair.

LUCINDA WAS NO LESS SHOCKED at Logan's aberration of mind than at his changed appearance. He appeared a ghost of his old stalwart, virile, giant self. And he forgot even the errands she sent him on. When he came home from down town she smelled liquor on his breath. She realized then, in deep alarm, that Logan had cracked. All his life he had leaned too far over on one side; now in this major catastrophe of his life he had toppled over the other way to collapse.

She had divined something of this upon his return, and had at once appealed to him to take her and Barbara back to Sycamore. If anything could save Logan it was action--something to do with his hands--some labours to draw his mind back to the old channels of habit. Before this blow, despite his sixty years, he had been at the peak of a magnificent physical life. If he stayed in Flagg, to idle away the hours in saloons and on corners, to sit blankly staring at nothing, he would not live out the year.

When the days had passed into weeks without his having done anything in regard to their return to Sycamore, she resolved to make the arrangements herself. She got Hardy to have a look at the big wagon, to grease the axles and repair the harness; and she hired a man to drive in the team and put them on grain.

Then she set about the dubious task of supplies and utensils. Al Doyle, who was as keen as Lucinda to get Logan out in the open again, declared vehemently: "There won't be one single damn thing left on that ranch. Logan forgot to leave a man on the place. All the tools, and furniture left in the cabin, will be gone. Stole!"

"Oh, dear me! Al, it's beginning to pioneer all over again!"

"It shore is. But that's good, Lucinda, 'cause it'll raise Logan out of this bog he's in... I advise you to take two wagon-loads. I'll borrow one for you, and hire a driver, an' I'll buy all the necessary tools, an' have them packed. The grub supply is easy to figure out. We'll put our heads together on the cabin an' the needs of you women-folk. Don't worry, Lucinda. It'll all be jake. The thing to do is to be arustlin'."

Only once did Lucinda's heart faint within her, and that was when she came home to 'find Logan and Barbara in the sitting-room, with little Abe crawling half naked and dirty around the floor. Logan was trying again to get some coherent response from Barbara. And she sat hunched in a chair, her great dark eyes the windows of a clouded mind. They struck terribly at Lucinda's heart.

She could not endure to stay there on the moment, so she went into the kitchen, where she grappled with fear and doubt. Was she mad to take these two broken wrecks back to the wilderness? Possible illness, accident, loneliness, Barbara's obsession to wander around, would be infinitely more difficult to combat down in the canyon than

in town. Here she could call in women or the
doctor. Despite the strong appeal of reason
supporting her fears, she succumbed to her first
intuition. If there were any hopes left for Barbara
and Logan, not to say bringing up the child, they
might rise down in Sycamore Canyon. The labour
did not appall Lucinda. Well she knew that upon
the pioneer wife and mother fell the greater
burdens. A strange subtle voice cried down her
misgivings. And with resurging heart she plunged
into the immediate tasks of getting ready.

They left Flagg with two wagons the next
morning before sunrise. Only faithful old Al Doyle
saw them off. His last words were--and they were
the last they ever heard him speak--"Wal, old-timer,
it's the long road again an' the canyon in the woods.
That's good. Adios!"

Lucinda rode on the driver's seat with Logan.
Barbara and the boy had a little place behind, under
the canvas. Evidently the movement, the grind of
wheels and clip-clop of heavy hoofs had excited
Barbara, who knelt on the hay to peer out with
strained eyes no mortal could have read. The
second wagon contained the farm tools, furniture,
and utensils.

After a while Lucinda's eyes cleared so that she
could see. She was glad to get out of Flagg. The
black stumps, the grey flats, the green lines of pines
and blue bluffs in the distance seemed to welcome
her. They had not quite reached the timber belt six

miles from town when Lucinda sustained a thrilling relief and joy in Logan's response to the winding road, the reins once more in his hands, the team of big horses, the rolling wheels, and the beckoning range. These had been so great a part of his life that only insanity or paralysis or death could have wholly eradicated them. They began to call upon old associations. Lucinda's loving divination had been god-sent. Logan's heart and spirit had been broken, and the splendid rush of his life at maturity had been stemmed, stagnated, sunk in the sands of grief and hopelessness. Her great task was to keep him physically busy until this ghastly climax of tragedy wore into the past. Life held strange recompense for the plodder.

Logan spoke at intervals, especially when they passed old camp-sites, now homesteads and ranches. Cedar Ridge, Turkey Flat, Rock Waterhole still existed in their pristine loneliness. Logan halted at the Waterhole for lunch and to rest the horses. Then he drove on till sunset, to stop at a small brook which drained into Mormon Lake.

They camped. The man they had hired for the trip turned out to be a helpful fellow, and between him and Logan, with Lucinda cooking, they soon had camp made and supper ready. Barbara walked around, her staring dark eyes as groping as her actions. She ate, fed the boy, and helped Lucinda. Sometimes she broke out into soft, hurried speech, half coherent, and again she stood gazing into the pine forest. Logan sat beside the camp-fire, but he did not smoke. Lucinda spread her blankets under a tarpaulin pegged down from the wagon-top and lay down with weary, aching body. The camp-fire sputtered, the wind blew--then while she was fearing the old lonely sounds, her eyelids closed as if with glue and she faded into oblivion.

Next day Logan made another long drive, to the deserted cabin half-way between the south end of Mormon Lake and Sycamore Canyon. Logan might not have even thought of their nearness to the old ranch, but Lucinda, during the supper tasks and afterwards, kept talking and asking questions until he became aroused.

Before noon the next day Logan turned off the main road at the end of Long Valley and drove down through the forest towards Sycamore.

What stinging beautiful emotions flashed over her as they passed the open glade where she had first seen Barbara playing with the boys! From then on, she was blinded by tears. They struck the down-grade. The old gate had not been closed since the cattle-drive. Logan emitted a strange hard cough, almost like a sob. He drove on, applying the brake. The wheels squeaked; the heavy wagon pushed the horses on. And then they reached a level.

"Same as always, Luce--just the same!" exclaimed Logan, huskily. "Only we are changed."

Lucinda wiped her eyes so that she could see to get off.

"Drive up to the cabin, Logan," she said, "and spread a blanket in the shade for Barbara and the baby...What shall I tell the teamster to do with his load?"

"Unload it, I reckon, here by the barn," rejoined Logan,' whipping his reins. "Gedap there!"

The helping hand arrived while Lucinda was looking around. The barn was stripped, proving how wise Al Doyle had been to advise a new outfit. Lucinda directed the driver to unload the farming equipment and pack it into the barn, then come on up to the cabin with the furniture.

That done, Lucinda turned to the old hollow-worn path. Her feet seemed leaden. There was a pang in her breast and a constriction in her throat. The joy she had anticipated failed to come at once. But she knew something would break the deadlock.

The brook was bank-full of snow-fed water, the old log bridge as it had been. Then she espied Logan. He had halted the wagon and was looking across at the unfinished stone corral. One look at his tortured visage was enough. The very stone Lucinda remembered seeing Logan put down on the wall sat there, mute yet trenchant with memory of the three sons who had helped build that wall with Logan, and who could not finish it because they had gone to war.

Logan drove on up to the cabin. Lucinda, lagging behind, fighting her own anguish, came to the long row of her sunflowers. They were blooming, great golden-leaved, brown-centered flowers, facing the sun. With sight of them the joy of home-coming flooded her being. She caressed the big blossoms and pressed them to her breast; then she found early golden rod and purple asters along the path. She gazed down the canyon for the first time. The high walls, the black ruins, seemed to gaze down protectingly upon her. Home! They assured her of that and they gave austere and solemn promise of the future.

Lucinda found the baby rolling and crawling on a blanket; Barbara, wildly excited by familiar scenes and objects that must have pierced close to reason, was running around in and out of the cabin. Logan was inside.

The flat flagstone lay under the hollowed log threshold. Lucinda knew both as well as her right hand. Wan bluebells smiled up at her out of the grassy margins. She peered into the cabin conscious of a clogged breast and pounding heart. Her emotions had not prepared her for practical facts. That cabin, hallowed by so much of sad and beautiful life, was a dingy, dusty, spider-webbed barn. The rude table and bench-seats and the old rustic armchair, relics of Logan's master hand so many years ago, were the only articles left inside. The bough-bed had been torn apart, no doubt for firewood; all the deer and elk horns and skins were gone from the walls. In places the yellow stones of the fireplace were crumbling. An Indian or some cowboy artist had drawn crude but striking images on the smooth surfaces.

Logan was cursing, which sounds for once Lucinda heard with delight.

"...---- ----dirty hole not fit for cattle. This here home of ours has been a camp for low-down hunters and loafers, and later a den for skunks, wildcats, coyotes, and Lord knows what else! There's a hole in the shingles. Some of the chinks are out between the logs. That door is hanging loose and won't shut. And dirt! Say, it's dirtier than all outdoors. Just one hell of a dump!"

"Yes, Logan--but home," rejoined Lucinda softly, as much overcome by his practical reaction as by the fact she expressed. "Huh! Home? --Aw, thet's so, Luce."

"I'll be practical, too, husband," said Lucinda, inspired to action. "Get out the broom and mop. And water buckets. And soap. We'll sweep and brush and scrape and scrub...Mend the hinge on the door. Have the driver put a canvas over the hole in the roof. Have him cut a lot of spruce boughs. After that's done you can unpack and carry everything in. After that, Logan, if you're able to, see if you can chop some wood."

"Hell! I can chop wood," declared Logan, in gruff resentment.

Lucinda set to work, and she kept the two men, and Barbara also, busy at various tasks. When Logan flagged and Barbara drifted off into space,

Lucinda prompted them again. They could not apply themselves for long. When sunset came, and at that season of early summer the golden rays shone through door and window, Lucinda surveyed the interior of the cabin with incredulous eyes and swelling heart. The den of hunters and beasts had been transformed. It was home once more, and more comfortable and colorful than ever before. Barbara had her old corner, where she sat on her bed with vague gaze trying to pierce a veil of mystery. Little Abe crawled around delighted with this new abode. Logan sat in his old chair, watching the fire, apparently lost to any of the grateful and beautiful feelings that stirred Lucinda.

Darkness stole up the canyon while she prepared supper. The night-hawks and the insects began their familiar choruses. A glorious rose and gold after-glow slowly paled above the western rim. The brook babbled as of old. Nature had not changed. Lucinda recalled the prayers of her youth. Her task was infinite, almost insurmountable, but her faith grew stronger. When night came, while she lay awake by Logan's side, with Barbara's corner silent as the grave, and the old wind-song mourning in the tips of the pines, then she seemed divided between hope and terror. In the hours when she wooed slumber she became prey to the past, to her early years here, to memory of her awakening to real love for her pioneer husband, to the coming of their first-born, to that terrible and fascinating

Matazel, to Abe's birth in a cow-manger, and so on through all the succeeding years of trial down to this agonizing end for the Huetts.

However, when morning came and the sun shone and the canyon smiled in its early summer dress, Lucinda did not fall prey to such memories. Her hope for the future battled with realism, with the thought of age and poverty, of her insupportable task with Logan and Barbara.

Night and day then for a week her mind worked from the somber to the bright, from the material fact to the spiritual belief, before she noted a gain for the latter. She grasped something to her soul that she could not explain. She no longer pondered over the inscrutable ways of God. She forgot the horror of war and the crawling maggots of men who fostered it. Her work lay here in this wild canyon and was still a long way from being finished.

Lucinda soon began her labors in the garden. About the only thing she could keep Logan steadily at was chopping wood. He seemed to enjoy that, and his swing of axe had much of its old vigor; but when she sent him to the pasture to bring in one of the horses, saddle and snake down dead aspen and oak to chop, he seldom materialized unless she hunted him up. Manifestly this was what she must do! Mostly she found Logan beside the old unfinished 'stone corral. At these sad times she hated to break in on his reveries, and some days she could not bring herself to this cruelty, and she left him alone with his memories. Nevertheless, it was forced on her to see that she must keep him working.

With Barbara she had less trouble. Barbara would obey as long as the idea of work lingered in her mind, but when sooner or later it faded, she would wander away. She always wanted to go into the woods. There seemed to be something beckoning to her off under the dark pines. She would sit by the door on the old porch bench and watch the canyon trail, a habit appearing to Lucinda to be the one nearest rationality. It had to do, Lucinda thought, with vague mind-pictures of Abe riding up the canyon. It was heart-rending to watch, but Lucinda found some inexplicable grain of hope in it.

Little Abe had improved and grew like a weed. Sometimes Barbara neglected to nurse him, but he never forgot when he was hungry. When Lucinda told Logan that they must have a milk cow very soon, Logan agreed, and almost instantly let the need slip from his mind.

Lucinda, with some help from Logan and Barbara, succeeded in planting her garden patch by the end of June. This time, in a normal season, was not too late to ensure a crop before the severe frosts came, and with their supplies and the meat she hoped Logan would provide they could live well through even a fairly severe winter.

"Logan," she said one night as he sat by the fire, "summer is getting along. You must snake down a lot of firewood and chop it for winter."

"Plenty of time, wife," he said. "Why, it can't be June yet."

"June has passed, husband," she replied patiently. "You should have all the wood cut and stowed before Indian-summer comes."

"Why ought I?"

"Because at that season you roam around the forest locating the game. Getting ready for your fall hunt! You forget. There never was anything you'd let interfere with that. We must have plenty of venison hung up and frozen, a lot of turkeys, an elk haunch or two--and some of those nice juicy bear-ribs that always pleased you."

She did not betray her intense hope for his reception of these suggestions. Long she had refrained from urging them. If he showed no interest--if he failed to respond...She dared not follow out her train of thought.

"Huntin' season! --By gosh, I never thought of that," he ejaculated, lifting his shaggy head with a flare of grey-stone eyes. She had struck fire from him and was overjoyed. Next instant he sagged back. "Aw hell! --Huntin' without Abe? --I don't know...I reckon I couldn't."

"Logan, you must feed Abe's boy so that he can grow up fast and hunt with you," replied Lucinda, sagely.

"My Gawd, Luce, do you expect me to live that long?" he asked, haggardly.

"Of course, I do."

"Humph. I reckon I don't want to," he said gloomily. But he seemed to be disturbed and haunted by the idea. "Wal, there won't be any game when little Abe gets big enough to pack a gun."

"You once said there would always be turkey and deer in the breaks of the canyons."

"That's so, Luce. I'll think it over...Have you seen my rifles?"

"Yes. I rolled them in canvas. And Al bought a new stock of shells."

"Ahuh...Doggone me!" he added mildly.

Lucinda wept that night while Logan slept heavily beside her. It was not from exhaustion and pain, although after she lay down, she could not move, and her raw, blistered hands and aching limbs hurt her excruciatingly, that Lucinda shed slow, hot tears. They were tears of joy at some little reward to her prayers for Logan.

But Logan never unrolled the canvas bundles of rifles which Lucinda leaned against the fireplace, nor did he take down the pipe and tobacco which she placed in plain sight on the jutting corner of the chimney, where he had always kept them.

Lucinda toiled on, unquenchable in faith that Logan would rise out of his gloom of despondency, and that Barbara was not permanently deprived of her sanity. If there were not daily almost imperceptible things to keep this hope alive in her, then she suffered under a delusion. Work was a blessing. It sustained Lucinda in this period which tried her soul.

One summer morning, towards noon, when the great forest was so still that a dropping pine-cone could be heard far away, Lucinda bent over her work at the table under the back window of the cabin.

Occasionally she looked out to peer down the brook at Logan, who sat beside the unfinished stone wall staring at space. He made a pathetic figure. All about him expressed the catastrophe in which the labor of a lifetime, fortune, comfort, his sons, his patriotism, his faith in man and God, had vanished.

Lucinda sighed. She had moments of despair, in which she had to fight like a tigress for her young. It was ever-present, the stark, naked fact; against which she had only mother love, an ineradicable faith, and a nameless, groundless hope. Yet in the last analysis of her terrible predicament she had the profoundest of all reasons to fight and never to yield, never to lose faith--the task of bringing up Abe's son. When gloom lay thick upon her soul she was carried ahead by that duty.

Barbara was outside on the porch, in her favorite place facing the canyon and the trail, and the fact that she was humming a little song to the boy indicated that she was in one of her placid states of apathy.

All at once Lucinda ceased her work to gaze out up the forested canyon. No differing sounds had caused this. She was puzzled. The brook murmured on, the soft wind moaned on, a stillness pervaded the canyon. The sun was directly overhead, as she ascertained by the shadows of the pines. Something had checked her actions, stopped her train of thought. It did not come from outside.

Suddenly a stentorian yell burst the silence.

"Waa-hoo-oo!"

That was Logan's hunting-yell. Had he gone mad? Lucinda became rooted to the spot. Then her ears strung to the swift, hard hoof-beats of a running horse. Who was riding in? What had happened? Logan's whoop to a visiting cowboy? It seemed unnatural. The charged moment augmented unnaturally. How that horse was running! His hoofs rang on the hard trail up the bench. A grind of iron on stone, a sliding scrape and a pattering of gravel--then a thud of jangling boots!

"Bab, old girl--here I am!" called a trenchant voice, deep and rich and sweet.

Lucinda recognized it; and her frightened heart leaped pulsingly to her throat.

Barbara's piercing shriek followed. It had the same wild note that had characterized Logan's, and above and beyond a high-keyed exquisite rapture which could only have burst from recognition.

"Abe! Abe!"

"Yes, darling. It's Abe. Alive and well. Didn't you get my telegram from New York? My God, I-- I expected to see you...but not-- not so thin, so white. Dad must be okay--the way he yelled. And... Aw, my boy! So, this is little Abe? He has your eyes, Barbara...Brace up, honey. I'm home. It'll all be jake pronto."

"Abe! You've come back--to me," cried Barbara, in solemn bewilderment.

Lucinda heard Abe's kisses, but not his incoherent words. She lost all sensation from her head down. Her body seemed stone. She could not move. Abe had come home, and the shock had restored Barbara's mind. Lucinda felt that she was dying: joy had saved, but joy could also kill.

"Mother!" cried Abe. "Come out!"

If Lucinda had been on the verge of death itself his call at that moment would have drawn her back, imbued her through arid through with revivifying life. She rushed out. There stood Abe in uniform, splendid as she had never seen him, bronzed and changed, with one arm clasping Barbara and the boy, the other outstretched for her, and his grey eyes marvelously alight.

"Doggone! Here we are again," Logan kept saying.

It was an hour later. The incredible and insupportable transport of the reunion had yielded to some semblance of deep, calm joy. Logan seemed utterly carried out of his apathetic self. Barbara had recovered her reason; there was no doubt of that. Spent and white, she lay back against Abe, but her eyes shone with a wondrous love and gratitude and intelligence. Lucinda knew herself to be the weakest of the four. She had just escaped collapse. The hope of this resurrection, though she had not divined it, had been upholding her for weeks.

"Abe, did anyone in Flagg or on the way out tell you what happened to your father?" asked Lucinda.

"No. I got in late, borrowed a horse and came a'raring...What happened?"

"He sold out to the army cattle-buyers. Thirty thousand and nine hundred, at twenty-eight dollars a head...They swindled him. Not one dollar did he ever receive of that money."

"Good God!" exclaimed Abe, furiously.

It was for Logan then to confess shamefacedly his monstrous carelessness and trust.

"Aw, Dad! --Then we're back in the old rut again?"

"Poor as Job's turkey, son," replied Logan, huskily.

"I don't care on my own account," said Abe, dubiously. "But for mother and Bab--it'll be tough to begin all over again."

"Darling, I needed only you," whispered Barbara.

Abe's return acted miraculously not alone upon Barbara. Logan hung around him as if fascinated; as if he could not believe the evidence of his senses. Lucinda knew they were all saved. The war had not impaired Abe physically. And spiritually she thought he was finer, stronger. Abe was of the wilderness. The old potent loneliness and solitude, the trails and trees, the cliff walls, and home with Barbara and his boy--these would soon blot out whatever horror it was that haunted him.

It seemed to Lucinda that while she watched with beating heart and bated breath, a slow change worked in her husband. He stared into the fire. A rumbling cough issued from his broad breast. Then he stood up, apparently seeing straight through the cabin wall. He expanded. His shoulders squared. His grey eyes began to kindle and gleam, and all the slack lines and leaden shades vanished ruddily from his visage. When Logan reached for the old black pipe and the little buckskin bag, and began to stuff tobacco in the bowl, then Lucinda realized she was witness to a miracle. She stifled a sob which only Barbara heard, for she came swiftly to Lucinda, whispering the very truth that seemed so beautiful and so distracting. Logan bent down to pick up a half-burnt ember, which he placed upon his pipe. Then he puffed huge clouds of smoke, out of which presently stood his shaggy, erect head, his shining face, his eagle look. Lucinda saw her old Logan

Huett with something infinite and indescribable added.

CHAPTER 3
MILLY FAYRE

The Thundering Herd (1925)

"Courage is tiny pieces of fear all glued together," proclaimed Irisa Hail. These words ring true in this story about Milly Fayre. Milly is a slip of a girl who has fallen in with buffalo hide hunters pursuing the last of the huge buffalo herds. Her situation is bleak as the lustful men discuss whether to gamble for her or simply share her between themselves. To say Millie is in an abusive situation is an understatement. After the men get into a gunfight to determine her fate, Millie overcomes her fear and escapes with a wagon and team of horses, only to find herself chased by Comanches.

This story will resonate with women in physically or emotionally abusive relationships. Leaving an abusive relationship is a terrifying experience with very real risks of physical harm and issues relating to children, finances, security, societal pressure and much more. Most experts suggest that a woman take the time to put together a plan before leaving. However, when a woman knows more abuse is coming, she may muster up the courage to flee and become her own personal heroine, even in the face of a buffalo stampede.

MILLY LOOKED BACK at the dark, ragged line of the timber from where she had come. The air was clearer that way. Movement and flash attracted her gaze. She saw animals run out into the open. Wild, lean, colored ponies with riders! They stretched out in swift motion, graceful, wild, incomparably a contrast to the horses of white hunters.

Milly realized she was being pursued by Indians. She screamed at the horses and swung the lash, beating them into a gallop. The lightly loaded wagon lurched and bounced over the hummocky prairie, throwing her off the seat and from side to side. A heavy strain on the reins threatened to tear her arms from their sockets.

It was this physical action that averted a panic-stricken flight. The horses broke from gallop into run, and they caught up with scattered groups and lines of buffalo. Milly was in the throes of the keenest terror that had yet beset her, but she did not quite lose her reason. There were a few moments fraught with heart-numbing, blood-curdling sensations; which on the other hand were counteracted by the violence of the race over the prairie, straight for the straggling strings of the buffalo herd. The horses plunged, hurtling the wagon along; the wind, now tainted with dust and scent of buffalo, rushed into Milly's face and waved her hair; the tremendous drag on the reins, at first scarcely perceptible, in her great excitement, began to hurt hands, wrists, arms, shoulders in a degree that compelled attention. But the race itself, the flight, the breakneck pace across the prairie, with stampeding buffalo before and Comanche Indians behind--it was too great, too magnificent, too terrible to prostrate this girl.

Milly gazed back over her shoulder. The Comanches had gained. They were not half a mile away, riding now in wide formation, naked, gaudy, lean, feathered, swift and wild as a gale of wind in the tall prairie grass.

"Better death among the buffalo!" cried Milly, and she turned to wrap both reins round her left wrist, to lash out with the whip, and to scream: "Run! Run! Run!"

Buffalo loped ahead of her, to each side and behind, in straggling groups and lines, all headed in the same direction as the vague denser bunches to the right. Here the dust pall moved like broken clouds, showing light and dark.

She became aware of increasing fullness in her ears. The low rumble had changed to a clattering trample, yet there seemed more. The sound grew; it came closer; it swelled to a roar; and presently she located it in the rear.

She turned. With startled gaze she saw a long, bobbing, black, ragged mass pouring like a woolly flood out over the prairie. A sea of buffalo! They were moving at a lope, ponderously, regularly, and the scalloped head of that immense herd crossed the line between Milly and the Comanches. It swept on. It dammed and blocked the way. Milly saw the vermillion paint on the naked bodies and faces of these savages as they wheeled their lean horses to race along with the buffalo.

Then thin whorls of rising dust obscured them from Milly's sight. A half mile of black bobbing humps moved between her and the Comanches. She uttered a wild cry that was joy, wonder, reverence, and acceptance of the thing she had trusted. Thicker grew the dust mantle; wider the herd; greater the volume of sound! The Comanches might now have been a thousand miles away, for all the harm they could do her. As they vanished in the obscurity of dust so also did, they fade from Milly's mind!

Milly drove a plunging maddened team of horses in the midst of buffalo as far as the eye could see. Her intelligence told her that she was now in greater peril of death than at any time heretofore, yet, though her hair rose stiff and her tongue clove to the roof of her mouth, she could not feel the same as when those lean wild-riding Comanches had been swooping down on her. Strangely, though there was natural terror in the moment, she did not seem afraid of the buffalo.

The thick massed herd was on her left, and appeared to have but few open patches; to the fore and all on the other side there were as many gray spaces of prairie showing as black loping blotches of buffalo. Her horses were running while the buffalo were loping, thus she kept gaining on groups near her and passing them. Always they sheered away, some of the bulls kicking out with wonderful quickness. But in the main they gave space to the swifter horses and the lumbering wagon.

The dust rose in sheets now thin, now thick, and obscured everything beyond a quarter of a mile distant. Milly was surrounded, hemmed in, carried onward by a pondering moving medium. The trampling roar of hoofs was deafening, but it was not now like thunder. It was too close. It did not swell or rumble or roll. It roared.

A thousand tufted tails switched out of that mass, and ten times that many shaggy humps bobbed in sight. What queer sensation this action gave Milly--queer above all the other sensations! It struck her as ludicrous.

The larger, denser mass on the left had loped up at somewhat faster gait than those groups Milly had first encountered. It forged ahead for a time, then gradually absorbed all the buffalo, until they were moving in unison. Slowly they appeared to pack together, to obliterate the open spaces, and to close in on the horses. This was what Milly feared most.

The horses took their bits between their teeth and ran headlong. Milly had to slack the reins or be pulled out of the seat. They plunged into the rear of the moving buffalo, to make no impression otherwise than to split the phalanx for a few rods and be kicked from all sides. Here the horses reared, plunged, and sent out above the steady roar a piercing scream of terror. Milly had never before heard the scream of a horse. She could do nothing but cling to the loose reins and the wagon seat, and gaze with distended eyes. One of the white horses plunged to his knees. The instant was one when Milly seemed to be clamped by paralysis. The other white horse plunged on, dragging his mate to his feet and into the race again.

Then the space around horses and wagons closed in, narrowed to an oval with only a few yards clear to the fore and on each side. Behind, the huge, lowered, shaggy heads almost bobbed against the wagon.

The time of supreme suspense had come to Milly. She had heard buffalo would run over and crush any obstruction in their path. She seemed about to become the victim of such a blind juggernaut. Her horses had been compelled to slacken their gait to accommodate that of the buffalo. They could neither forge ahead, nor swerve to one side or other, nor stop. They were blocked, hemmed in, and pushed. And their terror was extreme. They plunged in unison and singly; they screamed and bit at the kicking buffalo. It was a miracle that leg or harness or wheel was not broken.

A violent jolt nearly unseated Milly. The wagon had been struck from behind. Fearfully she looked back. A stupid-faced old bull, with shaggy head as large as a barrel, was wagging along almost under the end of the wagon-bed. He had bumped into it. Then the space on the left closed in until buffalo were right alongside the wheels. Milly wrung her hands. It would happen now. A wheel would be broken, the wagon overturned, and she . . . A big black bull rubbed his rump against the hind wheel. The iron tire revolving fast scraped hard on his hide. Quick as a flash the bull lowered head and elevated rear, kicking out viciously. One of his legs went between the spokes. A crack rang out above the trample of hoofs. The bull went down, and the wagon lifted and all but upset. Milly could not cry out. She clung to the seat with all her strength. Then began a terrific commotion. The horses plunged as the drag on the wagon held them back. Buffalo began to pile high over the one that had fallen, and a wave of action seemed to permeate all of them.

Those rushing forward pounded against the hind wheels, and split round them until the pressure became so great that they seemed to lift the wagon and carry it along, forcing the horses ahead.

Milly could not shut her eyes. They were fascinated by this heaving mass. The continuous roar, the endless motion toward certain catastrophe, were driving her mad. Then this bump and scrape and lurch, this frightful proximity of the encroaching buffalo, this pell-mell pandemonium behind, was too much for her. The strength of hands and will left her. The wagon tilted, turned sidewise, and stopped with a shock. An appalling sound seemed to take the place of motion. The buffalo behind began to lift their great heads, to pile high over those in front, to crowd in terrific straining wave of black, hideous and irresistible, like an oncoming tide. Heads and horns and hair, tufted tails, a dense, rounded, moving, tussling sea of buffalo bore down on the wagon. The sound was now a thundering roar. Dust hung low. The air was suffocating. Milly's nose and lungs seemed to close. She fell backward over the seat and fainted.

When she opened her eyes, it was as if she had come out of a nightmare. She lay on her back. She gazed upward to sky thinly filmed over by dust clouds. Had she slept?

Suddenly she understood the meaning of motion and the sensation of filled ears. The wagon was moving steadily, she could not tell how fast, and from all sides rose a low, clattering roar of hoofs.

"Oh, it must be--something happened--the horses went on--the wagon did not upset!" she cried, and her voice was indistinct.

But she feared to rise and look out. She listened and felt. There was a vast difference. The wagon moved on steadily, smoothly, without lurch or bump; the sound of hoofs filled the air, yet not loudly or with such a cutting trample. She reasoned out that the pace had slowed much. Where was she? How long had she lain unconscious? What would be the end of this awful race?

Nothing happened. She found her breathing easier and her nostrils less stopped by dust and odor of buffalo. Her mouth was parched with thirst. There was a slow, torrid beat of her pulse. Her skin appeared moist and hot. Then she saw the sun, quite high, a strange magenta hue, seen through the thin dust clouds. It had been just after daylight when she escaped from Jett's camp. Hours had passed and she was still surrounded by buffalo. The end had not come then; it had been averted, but it was inevitable. What she had passed through! Life was cruel. Hers had been an unhappy fate. Suddenly she thought of Tom Doan, and life, courage, hope surged with the magic of love. Something had happened to save her.

Milly sat up. She saw gray prairie--and then, some fifty yards distant, the brown shaggy bodies of buffalo, in lazy lope. The wagon was keeping the same slow speed. Milly staggered up to lean against the seat and peer ahead. Wonderful to see--the white team was contentedly trotting along, some rods in the rear of straggling buffalo. She could scarcely believe what she saw. The horses were no longer frightened.

On the other side wider space intervened before buffalo covered the gray prairie. She could see a long way--miles, it seemed--and there were as many black streaks of buffalo as gray strips of grass. To the fore Milly beheld the same scene, only greater in extent. Buffalo showed as far as sight could penetrate, but they were no longer massed or moving fast.

"It's not a stampede," Milly told herself in sudden realization. "It never was. They're just traveling. They don't mind the wagon--the horses-- not any more. Oh, I shall get out!"

The knotted reins hung over the brake, where she had left them. Milly climbed to the driver's seat and took them up.

The horses responded to her control, not in accelerated trot, but by a lifting of ears and throwing of heads. They were glad to be under guidance again. They trotted on as if no buffalo were near. It amazed Milly, this change. But she could tell by the sweat and froth and cakes of dust on them that they had traveled far and long before coming to this indifference.

Milly did not drive the horses, though she held the reins taut enough for them to feel she was there; she sat stiff in the seat, calling to them, watching and thrilling, nervously and fearfully suspicious of the moving enclosure which carried her onward a prisoner. Time passed swiftly. The sun burned down on her. And the hour came when the buffalo lumbered to a walk.

They were no different from cattle now, Milly thought. Then the dust clouds floated away and she could see over the backs of buffalo on all sides, out to the boundless prairie. The blue sky overhead seemed to have a welcome for her. The horses slowed down. Gradually the form of the open space surrounding the wagon widened, changed its shape as buffalo in groups wandered out from the herd. Little light tawny calves appeared to run playfully into the open. They did not play as if they were tired.

Milly watched them with a birth of love in her heart for them, and a gratitude to the whole herd for its service to her. No doubt now that she was saved! Nearly a whole day had passed since the Indians had seen her disappear, and leagues of prairie had been covered. The direction she was being taken was north, and that she knew to be favorable to her. Sooner or later these buffalo would split or pass by her; then she would have another problem to consider.

But how interminably they traveled on! No doubt the annual instinct to migrate northward had been the cause of this movement. If they had stampeded across the Pease, which had not seemed to her the case, they had at once calmed to a gait the hunters called their regular ranging mode of travel. Her peril at one time had been great, but if this herd had caught her in a stampede she would have been lost.

The stragglers that from time to time came near her paid no attention to horses or wagon. They were as tame as cows. They puffed along, wagging their big heads, apparently asleep as they traveled. The open lanes and aisles and patches changed shape, closed to reopen, yet on the whole there was a gradual widening. The herd was spreading. Milly could see the ragged rear a couple of miles back, where it marked its dark line against the gray prairie. Westward the mass was thick and wide; it was thin and straggly on the east. Northward the black creeping tide of backs extended to the horizon.

Milly rode on, escorted by a million beasts of the plain, and they came to mean more to her than she could understand. They were alive, vigorous, self-sufficient; and they were doomed by the hide-hunters. She could not think of anything save the great, shaggy, stolid old bulls, and the sleeker smaller cows, and the tawny romping calves. So wonderful an adventure, so vast a number of hoofed creatures, so strangely trooping up out of the dusty river brakes to envelop her, so different when she and they and the horses had become accustomed to one another--these ideas were the gist of her thoughts. It was a strange, unreal concentration on buffalo.

The afternoon waned. The sun sank low in the west and turned gold. A time came when Milly saw with amaze that the front leagues of buffalo had disappeared over the horizon, now close at hand. They had come to edge of slope on river brake. What would this mean to her?

When the wagon reached the line where the woolly backs had gone down out of sight Milly saw a slope, covered with spreading buffalo, that ended in a winding green belt of trees. In places shone the glancing brightness of water. Beyond, on a level immense plain, miles and miles of buffalo were moving like myriads of ants. They were spreading on all sides, and those in the lead had stopped to graze. The immensity of the scene, its beauty and life and tragedy, would remain in Milly's memory all her days. She saw the whole herd, and it was a spectacle to uplift her heart. While the horses walked on with the buffalo streaming down that slope Milly gazed in rapt attention. How endless the gray level prairie below! She understood why the buffalo loved it, how it had nourished them, what a wild lonely home it was. Faint threads of other rivers crossed the gray; and the green hue was welcome contrast to the monotony. Duskily red the sun was setting, and it cast its glow over the plain and buffalo, stronger every moment. In the distance purple mantled the horizon. Far to the northwest a faint dark ruggedness of land or cloud seemed limned against the sunset-flushed sky. Was that land? If so, it was the Llano Estacado.

Milly's horses reached the belt of trees, and entered a grove through and round which the buffalo were traveling. She felt the breaking of the enclosure of beasts that had so long encompassed her. It brought a change of thoughts. She was free to let the remainder of the herd pass. Driving down, behind a thick clump of cottonwoods she turned into a green pocket, and halted. Wearily the horses stood, heaving, untempted by the grass. On each side of Milly streams and strings and groups of buffalo passed to go down into the river, from which a loud continuous splashing rose. She waited, watching on one side, then the other. The solid masses had gone by; the ranks behind thinned as they came on; and at last straggling groups with many calves brought up the rear. These hurried on, rustling the bush, on to splash into the shallow ford. Then the violence of agitated water ceased; the low trample of hoofs ceased.

Silence! It was not real. For a whole day Milly's ears had been filled and harassed by a continuous trample, at first a roar, then a clatter, then a slow beat, beat, beat of hoofs, but always a trample. She could not get used to silence. She felt lost. A rush of sensations seemed impending. But only a dreamy stillness pervaded the river bottom, a hot, drowsy, thick air, empty of life. The unnaturally silent moment flung at her the loneliness and wildness of the place. Alone! She was lost on the prairie.

"Oh, what shall I do now?" she cried.

There was everything to do--to care for the horses, and for herself, so to preserve strength; to choose a direction, and to travel on and on, until she found a road that would lead her to some camp or post. Suddenly she sank down in a heap. The thought of the enormous problem crushed her for a moment. She was in the throes of a reaction.

"But I mustn't think," she whispered, fiercely. "I must do!"

And she clambered out of the wagon. The grove sloped down to the green bench where she had waited for the buffalo to pass. Grass was abundant. The horses would not stray. She moved to unhitch them, and had begun when it occurred to her that she would have to hitch them up again. To this end she studied every buckle and strap. Many a time she had helped round horses on the farm. The intricacies of harness were not an entire mystery to her. Then she unbuttoned the traces and removed the harness. The horses rolled in a dusty place which the buffalo had trampled barren, and they rose dirty and yellow to shake a cloud from their backs. Then with snorts they trotted down to the water.

Milly was reminded of her own burning thirst, and she ran down to the water's edge, where, unmindful of its muddy color, she threw herself flat and drank until she could hold no more. "Never knew--water--could taste so good," she panted. Returning to the wagon, she climbed up in it to examine its contents. She found a bag of oats for the horses, a box containing utensils for cooking, another full of food supplies, a bale of blankets, and lastly an ax and shovel.

"Robinson Crusoe had no more," said Milly to herself, and then stood aghast at her levity. Was she not lost on the prairie? Might not Indians ride down upon her? Milly considered the probabilities. "God has answered my prayer," she concluded, gravely, and dismissed fears for the time being.

In the box of utensils, she found matches, which were next to food in importance, and thus encouraged she lifted out what she needed. Among the articles of food were a loaf of bread and a bag of biscuits. Suddenly her mouth became flooded with saliva and she had to bite into a biscuit. There were also cooked meat and both jerked venison and buffalo. Salt and pepper, sugar, coffee, dried apples she found, and then did not explore the box to the uttermost.

"I'll not starve, anyway," murmured Milly.

Next, she gathered dry bits of bark and wood, of which there was abundance, and essayed to start a fire. Success crowned her efforts, though she burned her fingers. Then, taking up the pail, she descended the bank to the river and filled it with water, which was now clarifying in the slow current. Returning, she poured some into the coffee pot and put that in the edge of the fire. Next, while waiting for the water to boil she cut strips of the cooked buffalo meat and heated them in a pan. She had misgivings about what her cooking might be. Nevertheless, she sat down presently and ate as heartily as ever before in her life.

Twilight had fallen when she looked up from the last task. The west was rose with an afterglow of sunset. All at once, now that action had to be suspended, she was confronted with reality. The emotion of reality!

"Oh, I'm lost--alone--helpless!" she exclaimed. "It's growing dark. I was always afraid of the dark."

And she shivered there through a long moment of feeling. She would be compelled to think now. She could not force sleep. How impossible to fall asleep! Panthers, bears, wildcats, wolves lived in these river brakes. She felt in her coat for the little derringer. It was gone. She had no weapons save the ax, and she could not wield that effectively.

Yet she did not at once seek the apparent security of her bed in the wagon. She walked about, though close by. She peered into the gathering shadows. She listened. The silence had been relieved by crickets and frogs. Slowly the black night mantled the river bottom and the trains of stars twinkled in the blue dome.

The presence of the horses, as they grazed near, brought something of comfort, if not relief.

She remembered a dog she had loved. Rover--if she only had him now! Then she climbed into the wagon, and without removing even her boots she crawled into the blankets. They had been disarranged in the rough ride. She needed them more to hide under than for warmth. The soft night seemed drowsily lulling.

Her body cried out with its aches and pains and weariness, with the deep internal riot round her heart, with throb of brain. But gradually began a slow sinking, as if she were settling down, down, and all at once she lay like a log. It was too warm under the blanket, so she threw it back and saw the white stars, so strange, watchful. Finally, she succumbed to exhaustion and drifted into slumber.

CHAPTER 4

LUCY WATSON

From *Under the Tonto Rim* (1926)

Lucy Watson is a single social worker who travels alone to the backwoods country of Northern Arizona's Tonto Rim with a vague assignment to teach the families "to have a better home." Her parents have died and her sister eloped with a cowboy, leaving her free to pursue a career. She is well educated, having graduated from high school and normal school. (We assume this was Flagstaff's Northern Arizona Normal School prior to it becoming a university.) The young woman's choice to travel into the backcountry begs the question of whether she was heroic in doing so or simply spreading her wings like most young people who face the daunting task of leaving home and starting a new life.

Certainly, the first chapter of Under the Tonto Rim *(Page 3) suggests Lucy was making a heroic choice as she chats with the young brakeman on a train:*

The young brakeman came to her assistance and carried her luggage. "Goin' up into the woods, eh?" he queried curiously.

"Yes. I think they did say woods, backwoods," laughed Lucy. "I go to Cedar Ridge and farther still"

"All alone—a pretty girl!" he exclaimed."

"Do you think I need a--- a protector?" replied Lucy.

"Among those beehunters an' white-mule drinkers! I reckon you do, miss."

Assuredly, the backwoods of Northern Arizona were more rugged during the 1920s, when this story was set, than today. However, one can question whether simply moving to a new job is heroic. I argue that young people setting out on new lives make courageous decisions when they abandon the comfort zone of their early lives to pursue education and careers. Does this courage rise to the level of heroism? I'll leave that to your conjecture. However, you might be influenced by this quote from Holly A. Hartman, a social worker, regarding her chosen profession:

For those to whom this world seems to be a cold, cruel, and harsh place, we are the living proof that compassion, kindness, and caring are alive and well on this planet. We are their source of help and we are their beacon of hope. We are their heroes.

The story you are about to read only touches on Lucy's courage. To a greater extent, it provides a snapshot of the culture into which the young social worker has inserted herself. It tells of Lucy, a rough beekeeper named Edd (with two "d's) and a backwoods dance. The story offers a moment's comic relief from the previous traumatic stories of Betty Zane, Lucinda Huett and Milly Fayre. I hope it lightens your day.

Sisters of the Sage

THE SOLE TOPIC OF CONVERSATION

was the dance on Friday night. It expressed the wholesome and happy regard these youths and maidens held in the only recreation and social function that fell to their lot. Personalities and banterings were forgotten for the moment and other wonderful dances were remembered; conjectures as to attendance, music, ice cream, were indulged in. Presently, however, when they had exhausted the more wholesome reactions to this dance subject they reverted to the inevitable banter.

"Say, Dick, have you found a girl tall enough to take to the dance--one you wouldn't have to stoop 'way over to reach?" drawled Sam Johnson.

Dick's youthful face turned ruddy. The attention suddenly and unexpectedly thrown upon him caused him intense embarrassment. The prominent bone in his throat worked up and down.

"Boy, yore handy with tools," interposed Hal. "Make a pair of stilts for that fat little sister of mine yore sweet on. She's four feet eight an' weighs one fifty. Reckon you'd make Sam a' Sadie look sick."

Other sallies, just as swift and laugh-provoking, gave the poor boy no time to recover, even if he had been able to retaliate. It was his sister Allie who came to the rescue from the door of the kitchen.

"Sadie, who're you goin' with?" she inquired sweetly.

"Sam. He's the best dancer in this country," she announced.

"So, it's settled then," rejoined Allie casually. "When I asked him the other day who he was goin' with I kind of got a hunch it might not be you."

Sadie flashed a surprised and resentful look up at Sam. He took it, as well as the mirth roused by Allie's covert remark, with an equanimity that showed him rather diplomatic.

"Sadie, I told Allie you hadn't accepted my invite, which you hadn't," he said.

"Reckon it wasn't necessary," she retorted, in a tone that conveyed the impression of an understanding between them.

"Wal, Sadie," drawled Edd's slow, cool voice, "I reckon you'll find it necessary to hawg-tie Sam for dances--or any other kind of shindig."

This sly speech from Edd Denmeade gave Lucy an unexpected and delightful thrill. Almost she joined in the hilarity it stirred. Even the self-conscious Mertie burst into laughter. For a moment the tables had been turned; Sam was at a loss for a retort; and Sadie gave a fleeting glimpse of her cat-like nature under her smugness and pleasant assurance.

"Edd, have you asked any girl yet?" she inquired sweetly.

"Nope. Not yet. I've been away, you know," he replied.

"'Course you're goin'?"

"Never missed a dance yet, Sadie."

"It's gettin' late in the day, Edd," she went on seriously. "You oughtn't go alone to dances, as you do sometimes. It's not fair to break in on boys who have partners. They just have to set out those dances...Edd, you ought to be findin' you a regular girl."

Sadie's voice and face were as a transparent mask for the maliciousness of her soul.

"Shore, Edd," put in Sam, "an' you ought to hawg-tie her, too."

"Funny aboot Edd, ain't it?" interposed Gerd. "The way he can see in the woods. Say, he's got eyes! He can line a bee fer half a mile. But he can't line a girl."

"Nope, you're wrong, boy," replied Edd, with evident restraint. "Never had no trouble linin' a girl. But I haven't got the soft-soap you fellows use."

"Who are you goin' to ask to the dance?" insisted Sadie.

They nagged him, then, with this query, and with advice and suggestions, and with information that no matter what girl he asked he would find she had already accepted an invitation. It must have been their way of having fun. But to Lucy it seemed brutal. Almost she felt sorry for Edd Denmeade It struck her that his friends and relatives must have some good reason for so unmercifully flaying him.

For, despite the general bantering, they had made him the center and the butt of their peculiar way of enjoying themselves. The girl Sadie seemed the instigator of this emphasis thrown upon Edd, and Sam ably seconded her.

Amy Claypool, however, manifested a kindlier spirit, though she did not realize the tirade was little short of a jealous brutality.

"Edd, I'd ask the new schoolmarm," she said, lowering her voice. "She's awful pretty an' nice. Not a bit stuck-up."

Lucy heard this suggestion, and at once became a prey to amusement and dismay. Why could not the young people, and their elders, too, leave her out of all reckoning? Her pulse quickened with an excitation that displeased her. How her very ears seemed to burn!

Sadie Purdue burst into a peal of laughter. "Amy, you're crazy!" she exclaimed. "That city girl wouldn't go dancin' with a wild-bee hunter!"

This positive assertion did not produce any mirth. No doubt Sadie had no intention now of being funny. A red spot showed in her cheek. The sudden scrape of boots and clank of spurs attested to the fact that Edd Denmeade had leaped to his feet.

"Sadie Purdue, I reckon it's no disgrace to hunt bees," he said sharply.

"Who said it was?" she retorted. "But I've been among town folks. You take my hunch an' don't ask her."

Edd stalked off the porch, coming into range of Lucy's sight when he got down into the yard. His stride seemed to be that of a man who was hurrying to get away from something unpleasant.

"Sadie, you shore don't know it all," said Amy mildly. "If this home-schoolmarm wasn't a nice a' kind sort she'd not be up heah. Fun is fun, but you had no call to insult Edd."

"Insult nothin'," snapped Sadie. "I was only tryin' to save his feelin's."

"You never liked Edd an' you don't want anyone else to," returned Amy. "I know two girls who might have liked Edd but for you."

Lucy's heart warmed to this mild-voiced Amy Claypool. She did not make the least show of spirit. Sadie turned petulantly to Sam, and there was a moment of rather strained silence.

"Come an' get it, your birthday party," called Allie from the door.

That call relieved the situation, and merriment at once reclaimed the young people. Lucy was glad to see them dive for seats at the table. She was conscious of a strength and depth of interest quite out of proportion to what should have been natural to her. Still, she had elected to undertake a serious work among these mountaineers. How could she help but be interested in anything that pertained to them? But the wild-bee hunter! Quick as a flash then Lucy had an impulse she determined to satisfy. Would Edd Denmeade give these guests of his sister's the last bit of the honey upon which he set such store? Lucy felt that he ought not to do so and would not, yet she contrarily hoped that he might. There appeared to her only one way to ascertain, and that was to walk by the table and see. Despite her determination, she hesitated. Then fortunately the problem was solved for her.

Allie, sailing out of the kitchen door, set a pan rather noisily upon the table. "There's the last of Edd's honey. Fight over it!"

The next few moments' observation afforded Lucy the satisfaction of seeing the birthday guests actually engaged according to Allie's suggestion. From that scene Lucy formed her impression of the deliciousness of wild-bee honey.

Lucy did not lay eyes upon Edd Denmeade until late the following morning, when, after the visitors and school children had ridden away, he presented himself before her where she played with the twins on the porch.

"Mornin'. Reckon I'd like a few words with you," he said.

"Why, gladly!" replied Lucy, as she sat up to gaze at him.

Edd was standing down in the yard, holding his sombrero in his hands and turning it edgewise round and round. On the moment he did not look at her. Seen now at close range, with all the stains of that terrible ride home removed from garb and face, he appeared vastly different. He was laboring with thought.

"Ma a' pa have been tellin' me about you, but I reckon I'm not satisfied."

"Yes? Is there anything I can tell you?" said Lucy, relieved. She had actually been afraid he would ask her to go to the dance.

"Shore. I want to know about this here work you're goin' to do."

Then he looked up to meet her eyes. Lucy had never met just such a glance. His eyes were so clear and grey that they seemed expressionless. Yet Lucy conceived a vivid impression of the honesty and simplicity of the soul from which they looked. Whereupon Lucy took the pains to explain quite at length the nature of the work she had undertaken among his people. He listened intently, standing motionless, watching her with a steady gaze that was disconcerting.

"I reckon I can't figure that out so quick," he replied. " It's the way I feel. If you was goin' to live among us always I might feel different. But you won't last up here very long. An' suppose you do teach Liz an' Lize an' Danny a lot of things. They've got to grow up an' live here. They might be happier knowin' less. It's what they don't know that don't make any difference."

"You're terribly wrong, Edd Denmeade," replied Lucy with spirit.

"Ahuh! Wal, that's for you to prove," he returned Imperturbably. "I'll be goin' now. An' I reckon I'll fetch your outfit in about midday to-morrow."

Lucy stared after the tall figure as it stalked with a flapping of chaps keeping time with a clinking of spurs. Edd Denmeade was six feet tall, slender, yet not lean like his brothers. He was built like a narrow wedge, only his body and limbs were rounded, with small waist, small hips, all giving an impression of extraordinary suppleness and strength. Lucy had seen riders of the range whose form resembled this young bee hunter's. They had been, however, awkward on their feet, showing to best advantage when mounted on horseback. This Denmeade had a long, quick, springy stride.

When he had passed out of sight down the lane Lucy let the children play alone while she pondered over his thought-provoking words. She realized that he was right in a way, and that it might be possible to do these children more harm than good. But never if she could only impress them lastingly. The facts of the case were as plain as printed words to her. These backwoods people were many generations behind city people in their development.

In a fairly intelligent and broad way Lucy had grasped at the fundamentals of the question of the evolution of the human race. Not so many thousand years back all the human family, scattered widely over the globe, had lived nomad lives in the forests, governed by conditions of food and water. Farther back, their progenitors had been barbarians, and still more remotely they had been cave men, fighting the cave bear and the saber-toothed tiger. Lucy had seen pictures in a scientific book of the bones of these men and beasts. In ages back all the wandering tribes of men had to hunt to live, and their problems were few. Meat to eat, skins to wear, protection from beasts and ravaging bands of their own species! Yet, even so, through the long ages, these savages had progressed mentally and spiritually. Lucy saw that as a law of life.

These backwoods people were simply a little closer to the old order of primitive things than their more fortunate brethren of civilization. Even if they so willed with implacable tenacity, they could not for ever hold on to their crude and elemental lives. They could never evade the line of progress. Edd Denmeade's father was a backwoodsman; Edd himself was a bee hunter; his son would most likely be a forest ranger or lumberman, and his grandson perhaps become a farmer or a worker in the city.

Naturally this giant boy of the woods understood nothing of all this. Yet he had a quaint philosophy which Lucy felt she understood. In a sense the unthinking savage and the primitive white child were happier than any children of civilized peoples. In a way it might be a pity to rob them of their instincts, educate them out of a purely natural

117

existence. But from the very dawn of life on the planet the advance of mind had been inevitable. Lucy was familiar with many writers who ascribed this fact to nature. Her personal conviction was that beyond and above nature was God.

If Edd Denmeade was not stupid and stubborn she believed that she could enlighten him. It might be interesting to teach him; yet, on the other hand, it might require more patience and kindliness than she possessed. Evidently, he was the strongest factor among the young Denmeades, and perhaps among all these young people. Despite the unflattering hints which had fostered her first impression, she found that, after talking seriously with him, she had a better opinion of him than of any of the other young men she had met. In all fairness she was bound to admit this.

All the rest of the day and evening Lucy found the thoughts Edd had roused running in her mind, not wholly unsatisfying. Somehow, he roused her combativeness, yet, viewed just as one of the Denmeades, she warmed to the problem of helping him. Moreover, the success of her venture with this family no doubt hinged mostly upon converting the elder son to her support. Perhaps she could find an avenue open to her through his love of Mertie and devotion to the children.

Next morning found Lucy more energetic and active mentally than she had been so far. She had rested; the problem she confronted had shifted to a matter of her own powers. Nevertheless, neither the children, nor helping Mrs. Denmeade, nor reading over some half-forgotten treatises relative to her work, interested her to the point of dismissing Edd Denmeade from mind. Lucy realized this, but refused to bother with any reflection upon it.

She was in her room just before the noon hour when she heard Uncle Bill stamp up on the porch and drawl out: "Say, Lee, hyar comes Edd drivin' the pack-burros."

Denmeade strode out to exclaim. "So soon! Wal, it do beat hell how that boy can rustle along with a pack-outfit."

"Heavy load, too. Jennie looks like a camel," replied Uncle Bill. "Reckon I'll lend a hand on packin'."

Lucy quite unnecessarily wanted to run out to see the burros, a desire that she stifled. She heard the tinkle of their bells and the patter of their little hoofs as they came up to the porch.

"Wal, son, you must been a-rarin' to git home," drawled Denmeade.

"Nope. I just eased them along," replied Edd. "But I packed before sunup."

"Fetch all Miss Lucy's outfit?"

"Some of it had to be ordered. Sewin' machine an' a lot of dry goods. It'll be on the stage next week, an' I'll pack it then. Reckon I had about all I could pack to-day, anyhow."

"Say, Edd," called Allie's lusty voice from the kitchen, "who'd you go an' storm for the dance?"

"Reckon I haven't asked nobody yet," replied Edd laconically.

"You goin' to stay home?" rejoined Allie, her large frame appearing in the kitchen doorway. Her round face expressed surprise and regret.

"Never stayed home yet, Allie, did I?"

"No. But Edd, you mustn't go to any more dances alone," said his sister solicitously. "It makes the boys mad, an' you've had fights enough."

"Wal, you didn't notice I got licked bad, did you?" he drawled.

Allie went back into the kitchen, where she talked volubly in the same strain to her mother.

"Edd, reckon we'd better carry this stuff in where Miss Lucy can keep the kids out of it, huh?" queried Denmeade.

"I shore say so. It cost a lot of money. I hope to goodness she makes out with it."

Lucy heard his quick step on the porch, then saw him, burdened with bundles and boxes, approaching her door. She rose to meet him.

"Howdy! I got back pronto," he said. "Pa thinks you'd better have this stuff under your eye. Where'll we stack it? Reckon it'll all make a pile."

"Just set light things on the beds, heavy ones on the floor. I'll look after them," replied Lucy. "Indeed, you made splendid time. I'm very grateful. Now I shall be busy."

Sometime during the afternoon, when the curious members of the household had satisfied themselves with an exhaustive scrutiny of the many articles Lucy had in her room, and had gone about their work and play, Edd Denmeade presented himself at the door.

"Reckon I'd like to ask you something," he said, rather breathlessly and low.

"Come in," replied Lucy, looking up from where she knelt among a disarray of articles she had bought.

"Will you go to the dance with me?" he asked.

Lucy hesitated. His shyness and anxiety manifestly clashed. But tremendous as must have been this issue for him, he had come out frankly with it.

"Oh, I'm sorry! Thank you, Edd, but I must decline," she replied. "You see what a mess I'm in here with all this stuff. I must straighten it out. To-morrow work begins."

He eyed her with something of a change in his expression or feeling, she could not tell what. "Reckon I savvied you'd say no. But I'm askin' if you mean that no for good. There's a dance every week, an' you can't help bein' asked. I'm givin' you a hunch. If any schoolmarm stayed away from dances, folks up here would believe she thought she was too good for us."

"Thank you. I understand," replied Lucy, impressed by his sincerity. "Most assuredly I don't think I'm too good to go to a dance here, and enjoy myself, too."

"Maybe, then--it's just me you reckon you'd not like to go with," he returned, with just a tinge of bitterness.

"Not at all," Lucy hastened to reply. "I'd go with you the same as with anyone. Why not?"

"Reckon I don't know any reason. But Sadie Purdue was pretty shore she did...You wouldn't really be ashamed of me, then?"

"Of course not," replied Lucy, at her wits' end to meet this situation. "I heard you spoken of very highly by Mrs. Lynn at Cedar Ridge. And I can see how your parents regard you. At my home in Felix it was not the custom for a girl to go to a dance upon such slight acquaintance as ours. But I do not expect city customs up here in the woods."

"Reckon I like the way you talk," he said, his face lighting. "Shore it doesn't rile me all up. But that's no matter now...Won't you please go with me?"

"No," answered Lucy, decidedly, a little nettled at his persistence, when she had been kind enough to explain.

"Shore I didn't ask any girl before you," he appealed plaintively.

"That doesn't make any difference."

"But it means an awful lot to me," he went on doggedly.

It would never do to change her mind after refusing him, so there seemed nothing left but to shake her head smilingly and say she was sorry. Then without a word he strode out and clanked off the porch. Lucy went on with the work at hand, becoming so interested that she forgot about him. Sometime later he again presented himself at her door. He was clean shaven; he had brushed his hair while wet, plastering it smooth and glossy to his fine-shaped head; he wore a light-colored flannel shirt and a red tie; and new blue-jean trousers. Lucy could not help seeing what a great improvement this made in his appearance.

"Reckon you haven't thought it over?" he queried hopefully.

"What?" returned Lucy.

"About goin' to the dance?"

"I've been very busy with all this stuff, and haven't had time to think of anything else."

"Shore I never wanted any girl to go with me like I do you," he said. "Most because Sadie made fun of the idea."

This did not appear particularly flattering to Lucy. She wondered if the young man had really been in love with that smug-faced girl.

"Edd, it's not very nice of you to want me just to revenge yourself on Sadie," rejoined Lucy severely.

"Reckon it's not all that," he replied hurriedly. "Sadie an' Sam an' most of them rake me over. It's got to be a sore point with me. An' here you bob up, the prettiest and stylishest girl who ever came to Cedar Ridge. Think what a beat I'd have on them if I could take you. An' shore that's not sayin' a word about my own feelin's."

"Well, Edd, I must say you've made amends for your other speech," said Lucy graciously. "All the same, I said no and I meant no."

"Miss Lucy, I swear I'd never asked you again if you'd said that for good. But you said as much as you'd go some time. Shore if you're ever goin' to our dances why not this one, an' let me be the first to take you?"

He was earnest; he was pathetic; he was somehow most difficult to resist. Lucy felt that she had not been desired in this way before. To take her would be the great event in his life. For a moment she labored with vacillation. Then she reflected that if she yielded here it would surely lead to other obligations and very likely to sentiment. Thereupon she hardened her heart, and this time gave him a less kindly refusal. Edd dropped his head and went away.

Lucy spent another hour unpacking and arranging the numerous working materials that had been brought from Cedar Ridge. She heard Mrs. Denmeade and Allie preparing an early supper, so they could ride off to the dance before sunset. Lucy had finished her task for the afternoon and was waiting to be called to supper when again Edd appeared at the door.

"Will you go to the dance with me?" he asked, precisely as he had the first time. Yet there seemed some subtle change in both tone and look.

"Well, indeed you are persevering, if not some other things," she replied, really annoyed. "Can't you understand plain English...I said no!"

"Shore I heard you the first time," he retorted. "But I reckoned, seein' it's so little for you to do, an' means so much to me, maybe you'd--"

"Why does it mean so much to you?" she interrupted.

"Cause if I can take you, I'll show them this once, an' then I'll never go again," he replied.

It cost Lucy effort to turn away from his appealing face and again deny him, which she did curtly. He disappeared. Then Mrs. Denmeade called her to supper. Edd did not show himself during the meal.

"Edd's all het up over this dance," observed Mrs. Denmeade. "It's on account of Sadie's sharp tongue Edd doesn't care a rap for her now an' never did care much, if my reckonin' is right. But she's mean."

"Laws! I hope Edd doesn't fetch that Sally Sprall," interposed Allie. "He said he was dog-goned minded to do it."

"That hussy!" ejaculated Mrs. Denmeade. "Edd wouldn't take her."

"Ma, he's awful set on havin' a girl this dance," responded Allie.

"I'll bet someday Edd gets a better girl than Sadie Purdue or any of her clan," declared the mother.

A little while later Lucy watched Mrs. Denmeade and Allie, with the children and Uncle Bill, ride off down the lane to disappear in the woods. Edd had not returned. Lucy concluded he had ridden off as had his brothers and their father. She really regretted that she had been obdurate. Coming to think about it, she did not like the idea of being alone in the cabin all night. Still, she could bar herself in and feel perfectly safe.

She walked on the porch, listening to the murmur of the stream and the barking of the squirrels. Then she watched the sun set in golden glory over the yellow-and-black cape of wall that jutted out toward the west. The day had been pleasantly warm and was now growing cool. She drew a deep breath of the pine-laden air. This wild country was drawing her. A sense of gladness filled her at the thought that she could stay here indefinitely.

Her reflections were interrupted by the crack of iron-shod hoof on rock. Lucy gave a start. She did not want to be caught there alone. Peering through the foliage, she espied Edd striding up the lane, leading two saddled horses. She was immensely relieved, almost glad at sight of him, and then began to wonder what this meant.

"If he's not going to ask me again!" she soliloquized, and the paradox of her feeling on the moment was that she was both pleased and irritated at his persistence. "The nerve of him!"

Edd led the two horses into the yard and up to the porch. His stride was that of a man who would not easily be turned back. In spite of her control, Lucy felt a thrill.

"Reckon you thought I'd gone?" he queried as he faced her.

"No; I didn't think about you at all," returned Lucy, which speech was not literally true.

"Wal, you're goin' to the dance," he drawled, cool and easy, with a note in his voice she had never heard. "Oh--indeed! I am?" she exclaimed tartly.

"You shore are."

"I am not," flashed Lucy.

With a lunge he reached out his long arms and, wrapping them round her, he lifted her off the porch as easily as if she had been an empty sack. Lucy was so astounded that for an instant she could not move hand or foot. A knot seemed to form in her breast. She began to shake. Then, awakening to this outrage, she began to struggle.

"How dare you? Let me down I Release me!" she cried.

"Nope. You're goin' to the dance," he said, in the same drawling tone with its peculiar inflection.

"You-- ruffian!" burst out Lucy, suddenly beside herself with rage. Frantically she struggled to free herself. This fierce energy only augmented her emotions. She tore at him, wrestled and writhed, and then in desperation fraught with sudden fear she began to beat him with her fists. At that he changed his hold on her until she seemed strung in iron bands. She could not move. It was a terrible moment, in which her head reeled. What did he mean to do with her?

"Reckon I'll have to hold you till you quit fightin'," he said. "Shore it'd never do to put you up on Baldy now. He's a gentle hoss, but if you kicked around on him, I reckon he might hurt you."

"Let--me--go!" gasped Lucy hoarsely. "Are--you crazy?"

"Nope. Not even riled. But shore my patience is wearin' out."

"Patience! Why, you lout--you brute--you wild-bee hunter!" raved Lucy, and again she attempted to break his hold. How utterly powerless she was! He had the strength of a giant. A sudden panic assailed her fury.

"My God! You don't mean--to hurt me--harm me?" she panted.

"You dog-gone fool!" he ejaculated, as if utterly astounded.

"Oh! Then what--do you mean?"

"I mean nothin' 'cept you're goin' to that dance," he declared ruthlessly. "An' you're goin' if I have to hawg-tie you. Savvy?"

Whereupon he lifted her and set her in the saddle of one of the horses, and threw her left foot over so that she was astride.

"No kickin' now! Baldy is watchin' out of the corner of his eye," said this wild-bee hunter.

The indignity of her position, astride a horse with her dress caught above her knees, was the last Lucy could endure.

"Please let--me down," she whispered. "I'll--go--with you."

"Wal, I'm shore glad you're goin' to show sense," he drawled, and with action markedly in contrast to his former ones he helped her dismount.

Lucy staggered back against the porch, so weak she could hardly stand. She stared at this young backwoodsman, whose bronzed face had paled slightly.

He had bruised her arms and terrified her. Overcome by her sensations, she burst into tears.

"Aw, don't cry!" Edd expostulated. "I'm sorry I had to force you...An' you don't want to go to a dance with red eyes an' nose."

If Lucy had not been so utterly shocked, she could have laughed at his solicitude. Hopeless indeed was this backwoodsman. She strove to regain control over her feelings, and presently moved her hands from her face.

"Is there any place down there--to change--where a girl can dress?" she asked huskily. "I can't ride horseback in this."

"Shore is," he said gaily.

"Very well," returned Lucy. "I'll get a dress--and go with you."

She went to her room and, opening the closet, she selected the prettiest of the several dresses she had brought. This, with slippers, comb, and brush and mirror, she packed in a small grip. She seemed stunned, locked in a kind of maze. Kidnapped! Forced by a wild-bee hunter to go to a backwoods dance! Of all adventures possible to her, this one seemed the most incredible! Yet had she not been selfish, heartless? What right had she to come among such crude people and attempt to help them? This outrage would end her ambition.

Then hurriedly slipping into her riding clothes, Lucy took the bag and returned to the porch.

"Wal, now that's fine," said Edd, as he reached for the grip. He helped her mount and shortened the stirrups without speaking. Then he put a big hand on the pommel of her saddle and looked up at her.

"Shore now, if it'd been Sadie or any girl I know, she'd have gone in an' barred the door," he said. "I just been thinkin' that over. Shore I didn't think you'd lie."

Lucy endeavored to avert her gaze. Her horror had not faded. But again, the simplicity of this young man struck her.

"Do you want to back out now an' stay home?" he went on.

"You are making me go by force," she returned. "You said you'd hawg-tie me, didn't you?"

"Wal, reckon I did," he replied. "But I was riled an' turrible set on takin' you...Your havin' a chance to lock yourself in! Now you didn't do it an' I savvied you wouldn't."

Lucy made no reply. What was going on in the mind of this half savage being? He fascinated while he repelled her. It would have been false to herself had she denied the fact that she felt him struggling with his instincts, unconsciously fighting himself, reaching out blindly. He was a living proof of the evolution of man toward higher things.

"Wal, reckon I'll let you off," he declared at length.

"Are you afraid I'll tell what a brute you were?" she flashed sarcastically.

His lean face turned a dark red and his eyes grew piercing.

"Hell, no!" he ejaculated. "Shore I don't care what you tell. But I'd hate to have you think same as Sadie an' those girls."

"It doesn't matter what I think," she replied. "You'd never understand."

"Wal, I would, if you thought like them."

"Is it possible you could expect me to think anything but hard of you--after the way you treated me?" she demanded, with returning spirit.

"Hard? Reckon I don't mind that," he returned ponderingly. "Anyway, I'll let you off, just because you wasn't tricky."

"No, you won't let me off," asserted Lucy. "I'm going to this dance...and you'll take the consequences!"

At the corral gate Edd Denmeade swung his long length off his horse and held the gate open for Lucy to ride through.

"Wal, want to go fast or slow?" he asked as he mounted again.

"Prisoners have no choice," retorted Lucy.

Evidently that remark effectually nipped in the bud any further desire for conversation. His grey eyes seemed to be piercing her, untroubled yet questioning. He put his horse to a trot. Lucy's mount, without urging, fell in behind. His easy gait proved to be most agreeable to her. He was a pacer, and Lucy recognized at once that he was the kind of a horse it was a great pleasure to ride. He appeared to be eager, spirited, yet required no constant watching and holding.

The trail led into the forest, a wide, dusty, winding path full of all kinds of tracks, one of which Lucy thought she recognized as Dick's. She had noticed his enormous feet. Patches of manzanita, clamps of live oak, thickets of pine, bordered the trail. Above these towered the stately rugged-barked monarchs of the forest. The last of the afterglow of sunset flowed rosily on the clouds; through the green lace-work of trees gleamed the gold of the wandering wall above her. Shadows were lying low in the ravines headed away from the trail. Presently this level of woodland ended and there was a sharp descent, down which the trail zigzagged by easy stages. Then again, the forest appeared level. Lucy heard the dreamy hum of a waterfall. Here Edd took to a swinging lope, and Lucy's horse, as before, fell into the faster stride.

The forest grew darker and cooler. The trail wound in and out, always hiding what was beyond. Sometimes Edd's horse was out of sight. Lucy found herself in a strange contention of mind. Despite her anger and the absurdity of her being dragged virtually a prisoner to this dance, the novelty of the situation and the growing sensations of the ride seemed to be combining to make her enjoy them, whether she wanted to or not. That would be a humiliation she must not suffer. Yet no doubt the horse Baldy was the finest she had ever ridden. She had to fight herself to keep from loving him. Nor could she help but revel in this lonely, fragrant trail through the wild dales and glades. They rode out of levels and down steps, and crossed rushing brooks; and it appeared that Edd kept going a little faster all the time. Yet he never looked back to see how she fared. No doubt he heard her horse.

Twilight turned the greens and browns to grey. In the denser parts of the forest Lucy could scarcely see the dim pale trail ahead. Suddenly she caught a glimpse of a fire. It disappeared as she loped along, and then reappeared. Then, all too soon, she thought, they rode into a clearing dominated by a large low building, half logs and half rough boards. A fire burned brightly under a huge pine near the edge of the clearing, and it was surrounded by noisy boys and girls. Horses were haltered to saplings all around. Wagons and queer-looking vehicles attested to the fact that a road led to this forest school-house.

Edd halted at the rear of the building, and, dismounting, he set Lucy's grip on the ground and turned to help her off. But Lucy ignored him and slipped quickly down. She was warm, throbbing from the brisk exertion of riding, and in spite of herself not wholly unresponsive to the adventure.

"Wal, we're shore here," drawled Edd happily, no doubt keenly alive to the shouts of the young people round the fire. "You can dress in there."

He led her to a door at the back of the school-house. Lucy mounted the high log steps to enter. The room was bare, a small addition built against the building. There was no one in it, a fact that relieved Lucy. A lighted lamp stood on a table. On one side was a built-in couch covered with dried pine boughs. Besides these articles of furniture there was a box to serve as a chair.

Lucy closed the door and hurriedly set about the business of dressing. She was not in any hurry to go out to meet Edd and the people at this dance; but she found it expedient to do so, owing to the cold. The bare room was like a barn. Once dressed, Lucy rather regretted bringing her best and most attractive gown. She had selected it hastily and in a moment of stress. Excitement and exertion had left her pale, with eyes darker than usual. She could not spare time on her hair, but it looked the better for that.

"If this mirror doesn't lie, I never looked half so well," she murmured. "Now, Mr. Edd Denmeade, wild-bee hunter and wild kidnapper, we'll see!"

Lucy's mood did not tolerate the maxims and restraints she had set for herself. On the moment she was ready to abandon her cherished ambition to succeed in welfare work. Gorillas and outlaws and bee hunters were a little beyond her ken. Edd Denmeade had laid hold of her in a savage manner, to which the dark-blue marks on her white arms could attest. Lucy did not stop to analyze her anger and the limits to which it might drive her. One thing at least was clear to her, and it was that she would use all a woman's guile and charm to make Edd Denmeade rue this night. At first, she had intended to go straight to his father and mother and tell of the indignity that had been done her. But she had changed her mind during the ride, and now that she was dressed in her best her mood underwent further change. She had brought a light-blue silk scarf to go with her white gown, and throwing this round her bare shoulders she sallied forth. As she stepped down to the ground the bright blaze from the fire blinded her, yet she saw a tall dark form detach itself from the circle there and approach her.

"You shore dressed pronto," drawled Edd.

Lucy put her hand on his arm and walked beside him, perfectly aware of his long stare. He led her round the school-house to a front entrance, where another crowd of boys and girls whispered and gaped.

"Our old fiddler's late," said her escort, "an' I reckon the gang is rarin' to dance."

Edd had to push himself through a crowd just inside the door, and he did it in a rather imperative way. Once through this line, Lucy saw a large bare board floor, then a large room lighted by many lamps, and many people sitting and standing around the walls. Edd was leading her across the room toward a corner where there were a stove and a table. Here was congregated another group, including women and children. Mrs. Denmeade and Allie came to meet them; and if Lucy had wanted any evidence of creating a sensation, she had it now.

"Wal, ma, here we are," drawled Edd as coolly as if there were no strained situation. Perhaps for him there was none.

"For goodness' sake!" exclaimed his mother, in delight. "Lucy, I'm shore awful glad to see you here. You fooled us bad. That boy of mine is a fox."

Lucy's murmured reply did not include any of the epithets she might have laid upon Edd Denmeade. Allie appeared even more delighted to see her.

"Oh, it was good of you to come!" she whispered, taking Lucy's arm and squeezing it. "You look perfectly lovely. An' all the boys will die."

"I hope it'll not be so bad as that," laughed Lucy, softening unexpectedly. The warmth of her welcome and the extravagant praise of her appearance were too much for her. Whatever she felt toward Edd Denmeade, she could not extend to these simple, impulsive people. This was their social life, the one place they gathered to have pleasure, and here they seemed very different. Lucy was at once the cynosure of all eyes, and was surrounded by old and young alike. The twins, Liz and Lize, after their first blank bewilderment as at an apparition in white, clung to her with the might of conscious pride of possession. Denmeade and Uncle Bill greeted her with wrinkled faces wreathed in smiles. Lucy met Claypools, Millers, Johnsons, and numberless others whose names she could not remember. Edd brought young men, all lean, rangy giants, whom she could not have distinguished one from another. It dawned on Lucy that he wanted most of the boys there to meet her and dance with her. Indeed, he showed no selfish interest. But Lucy did not really look at Edd until Mrs. Denmeade, during an opportune moment, whispered to her:

"Lucy, I reckon Edd's the proudest boy in the whole world. Pa said the same. We never seen him this way before. He was never happy at our dances. But you've done him good by comin', an' I'm thankin' you."

Whereupon Lucy forced herself to gaze upon the escort who had gone to such an extreme to bring her to this dance. And she was to discern that, whatever his misconduct toward her, he was now wearing his laurels with becoming modesty. For Lucy could not blind herself to the fact that she was the star attraction of this dance, and that Edd had brought his rivals to a state of envy. Both circumstances pleased her. Seldom had she ever been the belle of a dance. Every young man who met her begged the privilege of dancing with her. And as introductions were quick and many, she could not remember names. How she enjoyed seeing Sam Johnson beg Edd for a dance with her! And Edd showed no rancor, no remembrance of insults, but with a courtesy that would not have ill become one in higher walks of life he gratified Sam. Lucy found the situation different from what she had anticipated. To revenge herself upon Edd Denmeade she had determined to be frigid to him and as sweet as she could make herself to every other boy there, particularly Sam Johnson. Not yet did she repudiate that unworthy resolve, though something was working on her--the warmth of her welcome--the pleasure she was giving--the honor she had unwittingly conferred upon this crude woodsman, the simplicity with which he took his triumph.

It dawned upon Lucy that there was only one reason why she could not thoroughly enjoy this dance, and it was because of what she called the brutal circumstances of her coming. Why had she not been willing and glad to come? Too late! The indignity had been perpetrated and she could not forget it. Nevertheless, she felt stir in her something besides the desire to shine and attract for the sole purpose of making Edd Denmeade miserably jealous. It was an honest realization that she could like these people and enjoy herself.

Commotion and stamping of feet and merry voices rose from the front of the school-house. Lucy was informed that the music had arrived. She saw an old man proudly waving a violin and forging his way to the tiny platform. The children screeched and ran for him. Edd joined the group with whom Lucy was standing. Then a loud twang from the fiddler set everyone to expectancy. When he began to play the couples moved out upon the floor. Edd said no word, but he reached for Lucy.

"Wait. Let me watch a moment," she said. "I want to see how you dance."

"Wal, shore we're no great shucks at it, but we have fun."

Soon the floor was half full of wheeling, gliding couples, with more falling in line every moment. Their dancing had only one feature in common with what she understood about dancing, and that was they caught the rhythm of the old fiddler's several chords.

"Very well, Mr. Denmeade, I think I can catch the step," said Lucy.

As he took hold of her it was not possible to keep from stiffening somewhat and to hold back. Still, she was to ascertain that Edd showed no thought of holding her closely. How serious he was about this dancing! He was surprisingly easy on his feet. At first Lucy could not fall in with his way of dancing; gradually, however, she caught it, and after several rounds of the room she was keeping time with him. It required a great deal of effort and concentration for Lucy to live up to her repute as a dancer. Manifestly Edd Denmeade did not talk while he danced. In fact, none of the dancers talked. They were deadly serious about it, and the expressions on different faces highly amused Lucy. She could not see that dancing held any sentimental opportunities for these young people. It seemed to Lucy a bobbing, gyrating performance, solemnly enjoyed by boy and girl in markedly loose contact.

Really, they danced wholly with their own intent and energy. Lucy found Edd's arm as rugged and unyielding as the branch of an oak. At last the dance ended, to Lucy's relief.

"Shore you can dance!" exclaimed Edd heartily. "Like a feather! If you hadn't leaned on my arm, I'd not have known you was there. New kind of dancin' for me!"

Lucy did not deign to reply. He led her back to the corner, where he found her a seat beside his mother. "Shore I hope you dance them all down," he whispered. "Reckon I wouldn't be in Sam Johnson's boots for a lot."

"What did he mean?" inquired Lucy of his mother, after he had left them.

"Dancin' anyone down is to make him give up--tire him out," she replied. "An' that about Sam Johnson is funny. Sam is reckoned to be the best dancer in these parts. An' so is Sadie. Wal, as everybody seen right off, Sadie can't hold a candle to you. An' Sam is goin' to find it out."

"Someone will surely dance me down," replied Lucy, with a laugh. "I am out of practice."

It developed that the time between dances was long, and given over to much hilarity and promenading around. The children took advantage of this opportunity to romp over the floor. Lucy soon was surrounded again, so that she could not see very much of what was going on. Sam Johnson claimed her for the next dance. He struck Lucy as being something of a rural beau, quite taken with himself, and not above intimating that she would surely like dancing with him better than with a big-footed bee hunter.

As a matter of fact, when the fiddler started up again Lucy found Sam's boast to be true. He was a surprisingly good dancer and she enjoyed dancing with him. But it was not this that prompted her to be prodigal of her smiles, and to approach audacity, if not actual flirtation, to captivate Sam. She did not stop to question her motive. He and his girl Sadie had been largely responsible for Edd Denmeade's affront to her. Yet Lucy did not dream that she was championing Edd. She had been deeply roused. The primitive instincts of these young people were calling to the unknown in her.

Once in the whirling maze of flushed faces Lucy found herself looking right into Sadie Purdue's eyes. Lucy nodded smilingly. Her greeting was returned, but Sadie failed to hide her jealousy and resentment.

When that dance ended Lucy was besieged by the young men, and gradually she gave herself up to the novelty of the occasion. Now and then she saw Edd dancing or attending someone, but he did not approach her. Mrs. Denmeade apparently took great pride in Lucy's popularity. The children gradually drooped and were put to sleep in the corner at the back of the stove. Lucy had to take a peep at them, some dozen or more of curly-headed little boys and girls, and several babies, all worn out with excitement and now fast asleep.

Dance after dance followed, stealing the hours away. By midnight, when the intermission and supper were announced by Mr. Denmeade, it seemed to Lucy that she had allowed her impulsiveness and resentment to carry her away. Sam Johnson had more than lived up to the reputation Edd had given him. Only Lucy's tact saved him from utterly neglecting Sadie; and as it was, he made a fool of himself. Mr. Jenks, the teacher, did not dance, and devoted himself to the older people. He had not found opportunity for more than a few words with Lucy, but several times she had caught him intently watching her, especially while she was with Sam. This, more than any other thing, made her reflect that perhaps she had already forgotten the ideal she had propounded to him. She suffered a moment of regret; then, when at the intermission Edd presented himself before her, cool and nonchalant, she could not help being rebellious.

"Wal, reckon I'll have to lick somebody before this night's over," he drawled as he led her across the room.

"Indeed! How interesting!" replied Lucy icily.

"Shore will, unless somebody backs down on what he said...Ma wants you to set with her at supper. Teacher Jenks has somethin' to say to you. Shore tickles me...Why, Lucy Watson, you've made this night the wonderfulest of my life! I've had enough dancin' an' gettin' even an' crawlin' of these here corn-huskers to last forever."

Lucy was afraid that for her, too, something wonderful lurked under the commonplaces of this experience, but she could not confess that Edd Denmeade had created it. She felt how little she was to regret that he had surprised her by not living up to the status of boor and ruffian. Instead of this he had turned out to be something approaching a gentleman. He became an enigma to her. It must be that he had no conception of his rude seizure of her person, his utter disregard of her feelings. Yet here at the dance he had eliminated himself, content to see her whirled about by his cousins and friends, simply radiating with the pride of being her cavalier.

"Reckon I'll help feed this outfit," he said, leaving her in a seat between his mother and Mr. Jenks.

"Well, I'd hardly have known you," said the school teacher with a smile and cordial greeting.

"Wal, I said the same," averred Mrs. Denmeade. "Shore she just looks lovely."

Lucy had the grace to blush her pleasure. "I declare this night will ruin my promise as a welfare worker. Too many compliments!"

"Not your promise, but your possibility," whispered Mr. Jenks significantly. "Young lady, I intend to talk to you like a Dutch uncle."

"Indeed, I hope you do," replied Lucy soberly. "Then I'll have something to tell you."

A corps of young men, among whom was Edd, passed round the room, distributing sandwiches and coffee, cake and ice cream. Soon the large hall-like place hummed with voices. Every seat along the walls was occupied. Around the entrance clustered a group of youths who had come without partners, and it was plain they felt their misfortune. Nevertheless, they had established some kind of rapport between themselves and other boys' partners. Lucy's keen susceptibilities grasped the fact that many of the girls welcomed this state of affairs.

Presently Mr. Jenks found opportunity to say, "You have created a havoc, Miss Lucy."

"Have I? Well, Mr. Jenks, I'm surely afraid that I wanted to," she confessed.

"I am not joking," he continued more earnestly. "Indeed, I make all allowance for a girl's natural vanity and pleasure in being admired. You are 'shore good fer sore eyes,' as I heard one old codger say. You have stormed this schoolhouse crowd. If looks could kill, Sadie Purdue would have had you dead hours ago. They all say, 'Sam is gone!'...It would be funny--if it were anything else but up in this backwoods."

"Oh, have I forgotten myself?" exclaimed Lucy aghast.

"Pray don't misunderstand," said Mr. Jenks hastily. "I think you very modest and nice, considering the unusual situation. But you have forgotten your welfare work. Of course, I don't see how you can avoid these dances. And that's the rub. Your popularity will make enemies among the girls and fights among the boys."

In self-defense Lucy related briefly and vividly how Edd Denmeade had seized her and held her powerless, threatening to tie her, until in her shame and fear she had consented to come to the dance.

"I'm not surprised," said Mr. Jenks gravely. "These fellows are built that way, and Edd is really what they call him, a wild-bee hunter. I believe that implies almost an Indian's relationship to the woods. But you must not mistake Edd and do him injustice. It never dawned on him that violence would be a profanation to a girl such as you...Could you honestly accuse him of the least boldness--you know what I mean?"

"No, I'm bound to confess that he handled me as if I were a boy or an old sack," replied Lucy honestly.

"Well, then, try to understand him. It will not be easy. He's a savage. But savages are closer to nature than other men, and somehow the better for it...What surprises me is that Edd has not made any fuss yet over Bud Sprall's attentions to you."

"Bud Sprall!" exclaimed Lucy with a start of amaze. "Have I met him?"

"Wal, I reckon," as Edd would say, rejoined the teacher, amused at Lucy's consternation. "You have danced twice with Bud, and showed that you liked it."

"Oh, but I didn't know," wailed Lucy. "I didn't catch half the names...Show him to me."

The school teacher managed presently, in an unobtrusive manner, to indicate which one of Lucy's partners had been the disreputable Bud Sprall.

"That handsome young fellow!" she burst out incredulously.

"Handsome, yes; Bud's good-looking enough and he can dance. But he is not just the fellow you can have dangling after you."

"I took him for one of the relations. There're so many. And I didn't see anything wrong with him except, come to think of it, he might have been drinking a little. But he was not the only one upon whom I detected drink."

"White mule! These boys will fetch a bottle to the dances. It's the one objectionable feature about their social family affairs. Naturally white mule kicks up fights."

"Oh, how unfortunate! How thoughtless of me not to know what I was doing!" cried Lucy.

"Don't be distressed," he returned kindly. "No harm yet. But I advise you to avoid Bud hereafter."

"I'm sure I promised him another dance," said Lucy in perplexity.

"Get out of it, then. And that's the worst of it. Bud will be sore and make trouble, unless you are very clever."

"Oh dear! How can I get out of a dance I've promised? And that Sam Johnson I was nice to him, deliberately. He's such a conceited fellow. I'm afraid I let him think he'd made a wonderful impression on me."

"Miss Watson, I have an inspiration," rejoined Mr. Jenks animatedly. "Confide in Edd. Get him to help you out of your dilemma."

"Edd! How could I? Impossible!" replied Lucy heatedly.

"Of course, that's for you to say. But if you don't, and cannot extricate yourself, I imagine you will only get in deeper."

Lucy, seeing Mrs. Denmeade approaching with friends, was unable to continue discussing the situation with Mr. Jenks. The parents of the children present were eager to talk to Lucy, and they asked innumerable questions. Before she realized the fleeting by of the supper hour the fiddler started one of his several tunes, and there followed a rush of dancers to the floor.

Edd did not exhibit any considerable alacrity in approaching her for this first number after the intermission.

"Want to dance this with me?" he queried coolly.

"Isn't it customary?" replied Lucy as she glanced over the dancers to select some she knew.

"Shore. But if you don't want to dance with me, I'd as lief not have you."

"Oh, really! Would you expect me to be dying to dance with you?" retorted Lucy with sarcasm.

"Nope. I'm not thinkin' about myself. But you think I am. My folks all reckon you're havin' the wonderfulest time. Wal, I hope so, but I've a hunch you're not. For I've been watchin' you. I saw you with Mr. Jenks."

"Really, it'd only be honest to confess that--that I'm enjoying myself--when I forget how I happened to come," said Lucy.

"So I reckoned. An' you can have this dance with anyone you want."

"But--you brought me here. Won't it look strange if you don't dance with me?" she queried with concern.

"Wal, the strangest thing that ever happened in this school-house was for a Denmeade's girl to dance with a Sprall," he returned bitterly.

"Oh! I am not your girl...And I had not the remotest idea I was dancing with Bud Sprall. I only just found out. Mr. Jenks told me."

"Say, you didn't know it was Bud Sprall you danced with twice?" he demanded, with piercing eyes of doubt.

"Absolutely no. I never caught his name," confessed Lucy.

"Wal, I'll be dog-goned! I wish everybody knew that. Shore I can tell my folks," he said ponderingly.

"Edd, I'm afraid I promised him another dance--after supper," went on Lucy nervously. She realized there was an undercurrent here, a force of antagonism quite beyond her. When his face turned white, she was nearer the truth. Abruptly he wheeled to leave her, but Lucy was quick to catch his sleeve and draw him back. The dancers crowded them to the wall.

"Do not leave me alone," she said swiftly. "Remember that I am a stranger here. You brought me against my will. I can hardly be blamed for dancing with Bud Sprall when I did not know who he was."

"Reckon that's all right," he replied, gazing down on her. "But you was sweet on Bud, an' you've shore turned Sam Johnson's head."

Lucy strove valiantly to keep her temper and find her wits. She began to have an inkling why Mr. Jenks was so concerned over her predicament.

"Suppose I was? Didn't you deserve to be punished?" she queried.

"Reckon I don't savvy you," he rejoined doubtfully. "Shore you strike me a little like Sadie Purdue."

"We are all women. Nevertheless, I don't consider that a compliment. But...you brought me here. I've made a mess of it. I was--well, never mind now. Only, it's your duty to help me not make, it worse."

"Who's sayin' I wouldn't help you?" he queried.

"You started to leave me."

"Wal, you said you'd another dance with Bud."

"But I didn't know who he was. Now I do know, I won't dance with him. I don't want to. I'm very sorry I blundered. But he seemed nice and--and---"

"Bud has a way with girls," said Edd simply, "Shore he's slicker than Sam."

"Will you take me home?" she asked urgently.

"Shore. But I reckon that'd make worse talk. You'd better stay an' let me take care of you."

"I--I'll do what you want me to," replied Lucy faintly.

"Wal, dance this with me. Then I'll hang around an' keep an eye on you. Keep out of that ring-around dance where they change partners all the time. When Bud or Sam comes up, you give me a look, an' I'll be there pronto. Shore all your dances are mine, an' I don't have to give any more to Bud or Sam."

"Thank you. I--I hope it turns out all right," replied Lucy.

While she danced her mind was active. She regretted her rash determination to make these crude backwoods youth jealous. He had certainly disappointed her in that regard. After awakening to the situation, first through her conversation with

Mr. Jenks and later with Edd, she realized she had jeopardized her welfare work. No matter what affront she had suffered; she should not have been so silly, so reckless, so undeserving of the trust placed in her. Yet what provocation! Her nerves tingled at the thought.

When the dance ended Edd relinquished her to one of his cousins, and gradually Lucy lost her worry for the time being. The next dance was the ring-around, which Lucy refused to enter, remaining beside Mrs. Denmeade. Here she had opportunity to watch, and enjoyed it immensely. The dancing grew fast and furious. When the dancers formed in a ring and wheeled madly round the room, shrieking and laughing, they shook the school-house till it rattled.

It developed that Edd Denmeade was more than a match for Bud Sprall when he presented himself for the dance Lucy had promised. But the interchange of cool speech struck Lucy keenly with its note of menace. Sprall's dark handsome face expressed a raw, sinister hate. Denmeade wore a laconic mask, transparent to any observer. The advantage was his. Finally, Sprall turned to Lucy.

"I ain't blamin' you, for I know you want to dance with me," he said. "Reckon I'll not forget. Good night."

Sam Johnson was not so easy to dispose of. Manifestly he and Edd were friends, which fact made the clash devoid of rancor.

"Wal, Sam, see here," drawled Edd finally. "You go an' fetch Sadie up. Reckon I'd like a dance with her. You've only had five dances with Miss Lucy. This here one will be six, if Sadie is willin' to trade off. So, fetch her up."

"Edd, I haven't got Sadie for this dance," fumed Sam. "Then you're out of luck. For I shore won't give up my partner."

Sam tramped away in high dudgeon. Lucy danced once round the room with Edd, and then joined the group outside eating ice cream beside the fire. Dawn was grey in the east. How dark the forest and mournful the wind! Lucy edged nearer the fire. She had become conscious of extreme fatigue, and longed for this unforgettable night to end.

Nevertheless, she danced until daylight. Her slippers were worn through. Her feet were dead. Never before in her life had Lucy expended such physical energy. She marveled at those girls who were reluctant to let the old fiddler off.

Lucy changed the white dress and slippers for her riding clothes. Though the morning was frosty, she did not feel the cold. How she could ever ride up to the Denmeade cabin she had no idea.

"Better get me on your horse before I drop," she told Edd.

He wanted her to remain there at the school-house with the children and girls, who were not to go home until evening. Mrs. Denmeade and Mrs. Claypool were getting breakfast for those who stayed. Lucy, refusing, was persuaded to drink a cup of coffee. Then Edd put her up on Baldy. All around the clearing boys and girls were mounting horses, and some of the older folk were driving off in wagons. Gay good-byes were exchanged. Lucy rode into the woods with the Denmeades.

At first the saddle and motion seemed a relief after such incessant dancing. But Lucy soon discovered that her strength was almost spent. Only vaguely did she see the beauty of the forest in the clear, crisp, fragrant morning. She had no sense of the stirrups and she could not catch the swing of the horse. The Denmeades trotted and loped on the levels, and walked up the slopes. Lucy could not have endured any one kind of riding for very long. She barely managed to hang on until they reached home.

The sun was rising in rosy splendor over the eastern wall. Wild turkeys were gobbling from the ridge behind the cabin. The hounds rang out a chorus of bays and barks in welcome.

Lucy almost fell out of the saddle. Edd was there beside her, quick to lend a hand.

"Wal, I reckon it was a night for both of us," he said. "But shore I don't want another like it, unless what I pretended was really true."

Murmuring something in reply, Lucy limped to her room, and barring the door she struggled to remove her boots. They might as well have been full of thorns, considering the pangs they gave her.

"Oh--oh--what a--terrible night!" she gasped, falling on the bed, fully dressed. "Yet--I know I wouldn't have missed it--for worlds...Oh, I'm dead! I'll never wake up!"

CHAPTER 5

LENORE ANDERSON

From *The Desert of Wheat* (1919)

WORLD WAR I WAS A DIFFICULT

TIME *for Zane Grey. The great author suffered frequently from debilitating depression and the war triggered his condition as he watched soldiers and sailors return from war injured, both physically and mentally. Grey found peers among the veterans living in the shell-shocked world we now call PTSD.*

In The Desert of Wheat, *the tragedy of war comes to the wheat fields of Washington State's Big Bend Country. Kurt Dorn, the son of a German-born wheat farmer, is brought home from the War on a stretcher, his body and mind shattered. Almost everyone believes his death is imminent, perhaps to be measured in hours and days... with the exception of Lenore Anderson.*

Lenore is the daughter of a wealthy wheat farmer. Her hand was promised to Kurt before he went to war. Too often relationships like theirs died when soldiers returned from battle missing body parts or too shell shocked to function as in the past. Lenore, chooses a more courageous path in which love and faith heal Dorn's body and mind.

"HE WILL DIE, AND THAT IS BEST FOR HIM,"

said the specialist. "There may be periods of rationality, but these, and perhaps periods of prolonged vitality, do not offer any hope. If he lives the night, he might be permanently impaired. He might be neurasthenic, melancholic, insane at times, or even grow permanently so.... It is very sad. He appears to have been a fine young man. But he will die, and that really is best for him."

The day following the specialist's visit Dorn surprised the family doctor, the nurse, Anderson, and all except Lenore by awakening to a spell of consciousness which seemed to lift, for the time at least, the shadow of death. Lenore could only gasp her intense eagerness and sit trembling, hands over her heart.

"I listened, and I peeped in," Lenore's sister, Kathleen shared. "Kurt was awake. He spoke, too, but very soft. I heard him say, 'Lenore'.... Oh, I'm so happy, Lenore—that before he dies, he'll know you—talk to you."

"Hush, child!" whispered Lenore. "Kurt's not going to die."

"But they all say so. That funny little doctor yesterday—he made me tired—but he said so. I heard him as dad put him into the car."

"Yes, Kathie, I heard him, too, but I do not believe," replied Lenore, dreamily.

Their father's abrupt entrance interrupted the conversation. He was pale, forceful, as when issues were at stake but were undecided.

"Kathie, go out," he said.

Lenore rose to face him.

"My girl—Dorn's come to—an' he's asked for you. I was for lettin' him see you. But Lowell an' Jarvis say no—not yet.... Now he might die any minute. Seems to me he ought to see you. It's right. An' if you say so—"

"Yes," replied Lenore.

"By Heaven! He shall see you, then," said Anderson, breathing hard. "I'm justified even— even if it..." He did not finish his significant speech, but left her abruptly.

Lenore was not aware of how she ever got to Dorn's bedside. But seemingly detached from her real self, serene, with emotions locked, she was there looking down upon him.

"Lenore!" he said, with far-off voice that just reached her. Gladness shone from his shadowy eyes.

"Welcome home—my soldier boy!" she replied. Then she bent to kiss his cheek and to lay hers beside it.

"I never—hoped—to see you—again," he went on.

"Oh, but I knew!" murmured Lenore, lifting her head. His right hand, brown, bare, and rough, lay outside the coverlet upon his breast. It was weakly reaching for her. Lenore took it in both hers, while she gazed steadily down into his eyes. She seemed to see then how he was comparing the image he had embedded upon his memory with her face.

"Changed—you're older—more beautiful—yet the same," he said. "It seems—long ago."

"Yes, long ago. Indeed, I am older. But—all's well that ends well. You are back."

"Lenore, haven't you—been told—I can't live?"

"Yes, but it's untrue," she replied, and felt that she might have been life itself speaking.

"Dear, something's gone—from me. Something vital gone—with the shell that—took my arm."

"No!" she smiled down upon him. All the conviction of her soul and faith she projected into that single word and serene smile—all that was love and woman in her opposing death. A subtle, indefinable change came over Dorn.

His eyes questioned sadly and wonderingly.

"You must be the great sower of wheat."

"Sower of wheat?" he whispered, and a light quickened in that questioning gaze.

"There will be starving millions after this war. Wheat is the staff of life. You must get well.... Listen!"

She hesitated, and sank to her knees beside the bed. "Kurt, the day you're able to sit up I'll marry you. Then I'll take you home—to your wheat-hills."

For a second Lenore saw him transformed with her spirit, her faith, her love, and it was that for which she had prayed. She had carried him beyond the hopelessness, beyond incredulity. Some guidance had divinely prompted her. And when his mute rapture suddenly vanished, when he lost consciousness and a pale gloom and shade fell upon his face, she had no fear.

From that hour, Dorn changed for the better. Doctor Lowell admitted that Lenore had been the one medicine which might defeat the death that all except she had believed inevitable.

Lenore was permitted to see him a few minutes every day, for which fleeting interval she must endure the endless hours. But she discovered that only when he was rational and free from pain would they let her go in. What Dorn's condition was all the rest of the time she could not guess. But she began to get inklings that it was very bad.

"Dad, I'm going to insist on staying with Kurt as—as long as I want," asserted Lenore, when she had made up her mind.

This worried Anderson, and he appeared at a loss for words.

"I told Kurt I'd marry him the very day he could sit up," continued Lenore.

"By George! that accounts," exclaimed her father. "He's been tryin' to sit up, an' we've had hell with him."

"Dad, he will get well. And all the sooner if I can be with him more. He loves me. I feel I'm the only thing that counteracts—the—the madness in his mind—the death in his soul."

Anderson made one of his violent gestures. "I believe you. That hits me with a bang. It takes a woman! … Lenore, what's your idea?"

"I want to—to marry him," murmured Lenore. "To nurse him—to take him home to his wheat-fields."

"You shall have your way," replied Anderson, beginning to pace the floor. "It can't do any harm. It might save him. An' anyway, you'll be his wife—if only for … By George! we'll do it. You never gave me a wrong hunch in your life … but, girl, it'll be hard for you to see him when—when he has the spells."

"Spells!" echoed Lenore.

"Yes. You've been told that he raves. But you didn't know how. Why, it gets even my nerve! It fascinated me, but once was enough. I couldn't stand to see his face when his Huns come back to him."

"His Huns!" ejaculated Lenore, shuddering. "What do you mean?"

"Those Huns he killed come back to him. He fights them. You see him go through strange motions, an' it's as if his left arm wasn't gone. He used his right arm—an' the motions he makes are the ones he made when he killed the Huns with his bayonet. It's terrible to watch him—the look on his face! … I heard at the hospital in New York that in France they photographed him when he had one of the spells.… I'd hate to have you see him then. But maybe after Doctor Lowell explains it, you'll understand."

"Poor boy! How terrible for him to live it all over! But when he gets well—when he has his wheat-hills and me to fill his mind—those spells will fade."

"Maybe—maybe. I hope so. Lord knows it's all beyond me. But you're goin' to have your way."

Doctor Lowell explained to Lenore that Dorn, like all mentally deranged soldiers, dreamed when he was asleep, and raved when he was out of his mind, of only one thing—the foe. In his nightmares Dorn had to be held forcibly. The doctor said that the remarkable and hopeful indication about Dorn's condition was a gradual daily gain in strength and a decline in the duration and violence of his bad spells.

This assurance made Lenore happy. She began to relieve the worn-out nurse during the day, and she prepared herself for the first ordeal of actual experience of Dorn's peculiar madness. But Dorn watched her many hours and would not or could not sleep while she was there; and the tenth day of his stay at "Many Waters" passed without her seeing what she dreaded. Meanwhile he grew perceptibly better.

The afternoon came when Anderson brought a minister. Then a few moments sufficed to make Lenore Dorn's wife.

The remarkable happened. Scarcely had the minister left when Kurt Dorn's smiling wonder and happiness sustained a break, as sharp and cold and terrible as if nature had transformed him from man to beast.

His face became like that of a gorilla. Struggling up, he swept his right arm over and outward with singular twisting energy. A bayonet-thrust! And for him his left arm was still intact! A savage, unintelligible battle-cry, yet unmistakably German, escaped his lips.

Lenore stood one instant petrified. Her father, grinding his teeth, attempted to lead her away. But as Dorn was about to pitch off the bed, Lenore, with piercing cry, ran to catch him and force him back. There she held him, subdued his struggles, and kept calling with that intensity of power and spirit which must have penetrated even his delirium. Whatever influence she exerted, it quieted him, changed his savage face, until he relaxed and lay back passive and pale. It was possible to tell exactly when his reason returned, for it showed in the gaze he fixed upon Lenore.

"I had—one—of my fits!" he said, huskily.

"Oh—I don't know what it was," replied Lenore, with quavering voice. Her strength began to leave her now. Her arms that had held him so firmly began to slip away.

"Son, you had a bad spell," interposed Anderson, with his heavy breathing. "First one she's seen."

"Lenore, I laid out my Huns again," said Dorn, with a tragic smile. "Lately I could tell when—they were coming back."

"Did you know just now?" queried Lenore.

"I think so. I wasn't really out of my head. I've known when I did that. It's a strange feeling— thought—memory … and action drives it away. Then I seem always to want to—kill my Huns all over again."

Lenore gazed at him with mournful and passionate tenderness. "Do you remember that we were just married?" she asked.

"My wife!" he whispered.

For days after that she was under a strain which she realized would break her if it was not relieved. It appeared to be solely her fear of Dorn's derangement. She was with him almost all the daylight hours, attending him, watching him sleep, talking a little to him now and then, seeing with joy his gradual improvement, feeling each day the slow lifting of the shadow over him, and yet every minute of every hour she waited in dread for the return of Dorn's madness. It did not come. If it recurred at night she never was told.

Then after a week a more pronounced change for the better in Dorn's condition marked a lessening of the strain upon Lenore. A little later it was deemed safe to dismiss the nurse. Lenore dreaded the first night vigil. She lay upon a couch in Dorn's room and never closed her eyes. But he slept, and his slumber appeared sound at times, and then restless, given over to dreams. He talked incoherently, and moaned; and once appeared to be drifting into a nightmare, when Lenore awakened him. Next day he sat up and said he was hungry. Thereafter Lenore began to lose her dread.

"Well, son, let's talk wheat," said Anderson, cheerily, one beautiful June morning, as he entered Dorn's room.

"Wheat!" sighed Dorn, with a pathetic glance at his empty sleeve. "How can I even do a man's work again in the fields?"

Lenore smiled bravely at him. "You will sow more wheat than ever, and harvest more, too."

"I should smile," corroborated Anderson.

"But how? I've only one arm," said Dorn.

"Kurt, you hug me better with that one arm than you ever did with two arms." replied Lenore, in sublime assurance.

"Son, you lose that argument," roared Anderson. "Me an' Lenore stand pat. You'll sow more an' better wheat than ever—than any other man in the Northwest. Look at facts like me an' Lenore. We gave you up. An' here you're with us, comin' along fine, an' you'll be able to do hard work someday, if you're crazy about it. Just think how good that is for Lenore, an' me, too.

Lenore eagerly watched her husband's face in pleasurable anticipation, yet with some anxiety. Wheat had been a subject little touched upon and the war had never been mentioned.

"Great!" he exclaimed, with a glow in his cheeks. ""Lenore, help me stand up," he asked, with strong tremor in his voice.

"Oh, Kurt, you're not able yet," appealed Lenore.

"Help me. I want you to do it."

Lenore complied, wondering and frightened, yet fascinated, too. She helped him off the bed and steadied him on his feet. Then she felt him release himself so he stood free.

"What do I say? Anderson, I say this. I killed Germans who had grown up with a training and a passion for war. I've been a farmer. I did not want to fight. Duty and hate forced me. The Germans I met fell before me. I was shell-shot, shocked, gassed, and bayoneted. I took twenty-five wounds, and then it was a shell that downed me. "

White and spent, Dorn then leaned upon Lenore and got back upon his bed. His passion had thrilled her. Anderson responded with an excitement he plainly endeavored to conceal.

"I get your hunch," he said. "If I needed any assurance, you've given it to me. To hell with the Germans! Let's don't talk about them anymore.... An' to come back to our job. Wheat! I got mad this summer. I bought about all the farms around yours up in the Bend country. Big harvest of spring wheat comin'. You'll superintend that harvest, an' I'll look after ours here.... An' you'll sow ten thousand acres of fallow on your own rich hills—this fall. Do you get that? Ten thousand acres?"

"Anderson!" gasped Dorn.

"Yes, Anderson," mimicked the rancher. "My blood's up. But I'd never have felt so good about it if you hadn't come back. The land's not all paid for, but it's ours. We'll meet our notes. I've been up there twice this spring. You'd never know a few hills had burned over last harvest. Olsen, an' your other neighbors, or most of them, will work the land on half-shares. You'll be boss. An' sure you'll be well for fall sowin'. That'll make you the biggest sower of wheat in the Northwest."

"My sower of wheat!" murmured Lenore, seeing his rapt face through tears.

"Dreams are coming true," he said, softly. "Lenore, just after I saw you the second time—and fell so in love with you—I had vain dreams of you. But even my wildest never pictured you as the wife of a wheat farmer. I never dreamed you loved wheat."

"But, ah, I do!" replied Lenore. "Why, when I was born dad bought 'Many Waters' and sowed the slopes in wheat. I remember how he used to take me up to the fields all green or golden. I've grown up with wheat. I'd never want to live anywhere away from it. Oh, you must listen to me some day while I tell you what I know—about the history and romance of wheat."

"Begin," said Dorn, with a light of pride and love and wonder in his gaze.

"Leave that for some other time," interposed Anderson.

Far up the slow-rising bulge of valley slope above the gleaming river two cars climbed leisurely and rolled on over the height into what seemed a bare and lonely land of green.

It was a day in June, filled with a rich, thick, amber light, with a fragrant warm wind blowing out of the west.

At a certain point on this road, where Anderson always felt compelled to halt, he stopped the car this day and awaited the other that contained Lenore and Dorn.

Lenore's joy in the ride was reflected in her face. Dorn rested comfortably beside her, upon an improvised couch. As he lay half propped up by pillows, he could see out across the treeless land that he knew. His eyes held a look of the returned soldier who had never expected to see his native land again. Lenore, sensitive to every phase of his feeling, watched him with her heart mounting high.

Anderson got out of his car. "I just never can get by this place," explained the rancher, as he came and stood so that he could put a hand on Dorn's knee. "Look, son—an' Lenore, don't you miss this."

Lenore looked first at Dorn's face as he gazed away across the length and breadth of land. Could that land mean as much to him as it did before he went to war? Infinitely more, she saw, and rejoiced. Her faith was coming home to her in verities. Then she thrilled at the wide prospect before her.

It was a scene that she knew could not be duplicated in the world. Low, slow-sloping, billowy green hills, bare and smooth with square brown patches, stretched away to what seemed infinite distance. Valleys and hills, with less fallow ground than ever before, significant and striking: lost the meager details of clumps of trees and dots of houses in a green immensity. A million shadows out of the west came waving over the wheat. They were ripples of an ocean of grain. No dust-clouds, no bleached roads, no yellow hills to-day! June, and the desert found its analogy only in the sweep and reach! A thousand hills billowing away toward that blue haze of mountain range where rolled the Oregon. Acreage and mileage seemed insignificant. All was green—green, the fresh and hopeful color, strangely serene and sweet and endless under the azure sky. Beautiful and lonely hills they were, eloquent of toil, expressive with the brown squares in the green, the lowly homes of men, the long lines of roads running everywhither, overwhelmingly pregnant with meaning—wheat—wheat—wheat— nothing but wheat, a staggering visual manifestation of vital need, of noble promise.

"Beautiful!" she replied, softly. "Like the rainbow in the sky—God's promise of life!"

"An' you, son?"

"As ye sow—so shall ye reap!" was Dorn's reply, strong and thrilling. And Lenore felt her father's strange, heart-satisfying content.

Twilight crept down around the old home on the hill. Dorn was alone, leaning at the window. He had just strength to lean there, with uplifted head. Lenore had left him alone, divining his wish. As she left him there came a sudden familiar happening in his brain, like a snap-back, and the contending tide of gray forms—the Huns—rushed upon him. for the thousandth time he re-killed his foes. That storm passed through him without an outward quiver.

"Lenore will never know—how my Huns come back to me," he whispered.

Then clearly floated to him a slow sweeping rustle of the wheat. Breast-high it stood down there, outside his window, a moving body, higher than the gloom. That rustle was a voice of childhood, youth, and manhood, whispering to him, thrilling as never before. It was a growing rustle, different from that when the wheat had matured. It seemed to change and grow in volume, in meaning. The night wind bore it, but life—bursting life was behind it, and behind that seemed to come a driving and a mighty spirit.

A soft footfall sounded on the stairs. Lenore came. She leaned over him and the starlight fell upon her face, sweet, luminous, beautiful. In the sense of her compelling presence, in the tender touch of her hands, in the whisper of woman's love, Dorn felt uplifted high above the dark pale of the present with its war and pain and clouded mind to wheat—to the fertile fields of a golden age to come.

Zane Grey

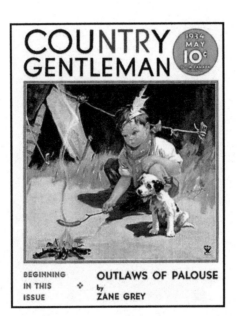

CHAPTER 6

EDITH WATROUS

Outlaws of Palouse (1934)

Outlaws of Palouse *is a story largely set along Idaho's Salmon River. The action revolves around horse rustling and mistaken blame.*

Integral to the tale is Edith Watrous, the daughter of a rancher who is a hellcat if there ever was one. She is a hopeless flirt who is unfaithful to the man to whom she is engaged. She also has a temper that can explode at a moment's notice, sometimes followed by heroic action.

In the story, Dale Brittenham is about to be hanged. He has falsely taken the blame for rustling a band of horses to protect Edith's fiancée. The tale begs the question of whether anger, courage and heroism are somehow connected one to the other.

St. Augustine, the Numidian theologian, suggested this may be the case way back in the early days of Christianity:

"Hope has two beautiful daughters. Their names are anger and courage; anger at the way things are, and courage to see that they do not remain the way they are."

TWO OF THE POSSE dragged Dale off the porch, and in a moment had bound him securely. Then Dale realized too late that he should have leaped while he was free to snatch a gun from one of his captors, and fought it out. He had not taken seriously Bayne's threat to hang him. But he saw now that unless a miracle came to pass, he was doomed.

The thought was so appalling that it clamped him momentarily in an icy terror. Edith was at the back of that emotion. He had faced death before without flinching, but to be hanged while Edith was there, possibly a witness—that would be too horrible. Yet he read it in the hard visages of Bayne and his men. By a tremendous effort he succeeded in getting hold of himself.

"Bayne, this job is not law," he expostulated. "It's revenge. When my innocence is proved, you'll be in a tight fix."

"Innocence! Hell, man, didn't you confess your guilt?" ejaculated Bayne. "Stafford heard you, same as Watrous an' his friends."

"All the same, that was a lie."

"Aw, it was? My Gawd, man, but you take chances with your life! An' what'd you lie for?"

"I lied for Edith Watrous."

Bayne stared incredulously and then he guffawed. He turned to his men.

"Reckon we better shet off his wind. The man's plumb loco."

From behind Dale a noose, thrown by a lanky cowboy, sailed and widened to encircle his head, and to be drawn tight. The hard knot came just under Dale's chin and shut off the hoarse cry that formed involuntarily.

"Over thet limb, fellers," called out Bayne briskly, pointing to a spreading branch of a pine tree some few yards farther out. Dale was dragged under it. The loose end of the rope was thrown over the branch, to fall into eager hands.

"Dirty business, Bayne, you—!" shouted Rogers, shaken by horror and wrath. "So, help me Gawd, you'll rue it!"

Bayne leaped malignantly, plainly in the grip of passion too strong for reason.

"Thar's five thousand dollars' reward wrapped up in this wild-hoss hunter's hide, an' I ain't takin' any chance of losin' it."

Dale forced a strangled utterance. "Bayne...I'll double that...if you'll arrest me...give...fair trial."

"Haw! Haw! Wal, listen to our ragged hoss thief talk big money."

"Boss, he ain't got two bits...We're wastin' time."

"Swing him, fellers!"

Four or five men stretched the rope and had lifted Dale to his toes when a piercing shriek from the cabin startled them so violently that they let him down again. Edith Watrous came flying out, half-dressed, her hair down, her face blanched. Her white blouse fluttered in her hand as she ran, barefooted, across the grass.

"Merciful heaven! Dale! That rope!" she screamed, and as the shock of realization came, she dropped her blouse to the ground and stood stricken before the staring men, her bare round arms and lovely shoulders shining white in the sunlight. Her eyes darkened, dilated, enlarged as her consciousness grasped the significance here, and then fixed in terror.

Dale's ghastly sense of death faded. This girl would save him. A dozen Baynes could not contend with Edith Watrous, once she was roused.

"Edith, they were about...to hang me."

"Hang you?" she cried, suddenly galvanized. "These men...Bayne?"

Leaping red blood burned out the pallor of her face. It swept away in a wave, leaving her whiter than before, and with eyes like coals of living fire.

"Miss Watrous. What you...doin' here?" queried Bayne, halting, confused by this apparition.

"I'm here—not quite too late," she replied, as if to herself, and a ring of certainty in her voice followed hard on the tremulous evidence of her thought.

"Kinda queer—meetin' you up here in this outlaw den," went on Bayne with a nervous cough.

"Bayne...I remember," she said ponderingly, ignoring his statement. "The gossip linking Dale's name with this horse-thief outfit. Your intent to arrest Dale!...His drawing on you! His strange acceptance of the accusation!"

"Nothin' strange about thet, Miss," rejoined Bayne brusquely. "Your lover was caught in a trap. An' like a wolf, he bit back."

"That confession had to do with me, Mr. Bayne," she retorted.

"So he said. But I ain't disregardin' same."

"You are not arresting him," she asserted swiftly.

"Nope, I ain't."

"But didn't you let him explain?" she queried.

"I didn't want no cock-an'-bull explainin' from him or this doubtful pard of his here, Rogers...I'll just hang Brittenham an' let Rogers talk afterwards. Reckon he'll not have much to say then."

"So, that's your plan, you miserable thick-headed skunk of a sheriff?" she exclaimed in lashing scorn. She swept her flaming eyes from Bayne to his posse, all of whom appeared uneasy over this interruption. "Pickens! Hall...Jason...Pike! And some more hard nuts from Salmon. Why, if you were honest yourself, you'd arrest them. My father could put Pickens in jail...Bayne, your crew of a posse reflects suspiciously on you."

"Wal, I ain't carin' for what you think. It's plain to me you've took powerful with this hoss thief an' I reckon thet reflects suspicions on you, Miss," rejoined Bayne, galled to recrimination.

A scarlet blush wiped out the whiteness of Edith's neck and face. She burned with shame and fury. That seemed to remind her of herself, of her half-dressed state, and she bent to pick up her blouse. When she rose to slip her arms through the garment, she was pale again. She forgot to button it.

"You dare not hang Brittenham."

"Wal, lady, I just do," he declared, but he was weakening somehow.

"You shall not!"

"Better go indoors, Miss. It ain't pleasant to see a man hang an' kick an' swell an' grow black in the face."

Bayne had no conception of the passion and courage of a woman. He blundered into the very speeches that made Edith a lioness.

"Take that rope off his neck," she commanded, as a queen might have to her lieges.

The members of the posse shifted from one foot to the other, and betrayed that they would have looked to their leader had they been able to remove their fascinated gaze from this girl. Pickens, the nearest to her, moved back a step, holding his rifle muzzle up. The freckles stood out awkwardly on his dirty white face.

"Give me that rifle," she cried hotly, and she leaped to snatch at it. Pickens held on, his visage a study in consternation and alarm. Edith let go with one hand and struck him a staggering blow with her fist. Then she fought him for the weapon. Bang! It belched fire and smoke up into the tree. She jerked it away from him, and leaping back, she worked the lever with a swift precision that proved her familiarity with firearms. Without aiming, she shot at Pickens's feet. Dale saw the bullet strike up dust between them. Pickens leaped with a wild yell and fled.

Edith whirled upon Bayne. She was magnificent in her rage. Such a thing as fear of these men was as far from her as if she had never experienced such an emotion. Again, she worked the action of the rifle. She held it low at Bayne and pulled the trigger. Bang! The bullet sped between his legs, and burned the left one, which flinched as the man called, "Hyar! Stop thet, you fool woman. You'll kill somebody!"

"Bayne, I'll kill you if you try to hang Brittenham," she replied, her voice ringing high-keyed but level and cold. "Take that noose off his neck!"

The frightened sheriff made haste to comply.

"Now untie him!"

"Help me hyar—somebody," snarled Bayne, turning Dale around to tear at the rope. "My Gawd, what's this range comin' to when wild women bust loose? The luck! We can't shoot her! We can't rope Jim Watrous's girl!"

"Boss, I reckon it may be jist as well," replied the lean gray man who was helping him, "'cause it wasn't regular."

"You men! Put away your guns," ordered Edith. "I wouldn't hesitate to shoot any one of you...Now, listen, all of you...Brittenham is no horse thief. He is a man who sacrificed his name...his honor, for his friend—and because he thought I loved that fiend. Leale Hildrith who was a treacherous spy—the go-between, a liar who deceived my father and me. Dale took his guilt. I never believed it. I followed Dale to Halsey. Hildrith followed me. There we found Ed Reed and his outfit selling Watrous horses. I recognized my own horse, Dick, and I accused Reed. He betrayed Hildrith right there and kidnapped us both, and rode to his hole...We got here last night. Reed took me before Bill Mason. Big Bill, who is leader of this band. They sent for Hildrith. And Mason shot him. Reed made off with me, intending to leave. But Dale had trailed us, and he killed Reed. Then he fetched me here to this cabin...You have my word. I swear this is the truth."

"Wal, I'll be...!" ejaculated Bayne, who had grown so obsessed by Edith's story that he had forgotten to untie Dale.

Dale frantically unwound the rope which Bayne had suddenly let go. Freeing himself, Dale leaped to Edith, who had dropped the rifle and stood unsteadily, her eyes wild.

185

"Edith, come, I'll take you in," said Dale, putting his arm around the weakening girl.

Zane Grey

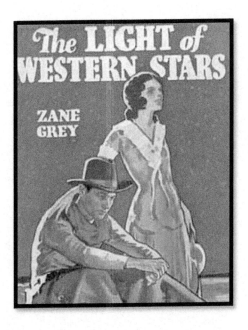

CHAPTER 7

MAJESTY HAMMOND

The Light of the Western Stars (1914)

MANY OF ZANE GREY'S characters *were young socialites who travelled west on trains to visit a relative who owns a ranch. Often these girls were flighty, flirtatious and excited to attract the eye of local cowboy. In The Light of the Western Stars, you meet "Majesty" Hammond, very different from these girls-- confident, competent and courageous.*

Majesty is a beautiful heiress who arrives at a western train station looking for her brother, Al. Al owns a small ranch with a huge burden of debt. Madeline pays her brother's debts with part of her inheritance, then falls in love with ranching. Enjoy what happens when she decides to buy her own ranch from an old cattleman named Stillwell who agrees to stay on and help her run the operation... if she can land an unruly cowboy as her foreman.

This story is only one of exciting tales in the book. For example, the final chapter of The Light of the Western Stars tells one of the greatest "race against time" tales in any Western novel. Make sure you buy the book if for no reason other than enjoying the thrilling culmination of the story.

FIVE MONTHS BROUGHT all that Stillwell had dreamed of, and so many more changes and improvements and innovations that it was as if a magic touch had transformed the old ranch. The April sun shone down upon a slow-rising green knoll that nestled in the lee of the foothills, and seemed to center bright rays upon the long ranch-house, which gleamed snow-white from the level summit.

Green slopes led all the way down to where new adobe barns and sheds had been erected, and wide corrals stretched high-barred fences down to the great squares of alfalfa gently inclining to the gray of the valley. The bottom of a dammed-up hollow shone brightly with its slowly increasing acreage of water, upon which thousands of migratory wildfowl whirred and splashed and squawked, as if reluctant to leave this cool, wet surprise so new in the long desert journey to the northland.

Quarters for the cowboys—comfortable, roomy adobe houses that not even the lamest cowboy dared describe as crampy bunks—stood in a row upon a long bench of ground above the lake. And down to the edge of the valley the cluster of Mexican habitations and the little church showed the touch of the same renewing hand.

Madeline Hammond cherished a fancy that the transformation she had wrought and in the people with whom she had surrounded herself, great as that transformation had been, was as nothing compared to the one wrought in herself. She had found an object in life. She was busy, she worked with her hands as well as mind, yet she seemed to have more time to read and think and study and idle and dream than ever before. She had seen her brother through his difficulties, on the road to all the success and prosperity that he cared for.

Madeline had been a conscientious student of ranching and an apt pupil of Stillwell. The old cattleman, in his simplicity, gave her the place in his heart that was meant for the daughter he had never had. His pride in her, Madeline thought, was beyond reason or belief or words to tell. Under his guidance, the lady ranch owner had studied the life and work of the cowboys.

She had camped on the open range, slept under the blinking stars, ridden forty miles a day in the face of dust and wind. She had taken two wonderful trips down into the desert—one trip to Chiricahua, and from there across the waste of sand and rock and alkali and cactus to the Mexican borderline; and the other through the Aravaipa Valley, with its deep, red-walled canyons and wild fastnesses.

This breaking-in, this training into Western ways, though she had been a so-called outdoor girl, had required great effort and severe pain; but the education, now past its grades, had become a labor of love. She had perfect health, abounding spirits. She was so active that she had to train herself into taking the midday siesta, a custom of the country and imperative during the hot summer months. Sometimes she looked in her mirror and laughed with sheer joy at sight of the lithe, audacious, brown-faced, flashing-eyed creature reflected there. It was not so much joy in her beauty as sheer joy of life. Eastern critics had called her beautiful in those days when she had been pale and slender and proud and cold. She laughed. If they could only see her now! From the tip of her golden head to her feet she was alive, pulsating, on fire.

No slight task indeed was it to oversee the many business details of Her Majesty's Rancho and to keep a record of them. Madeline found the course of business training upon which her father had insisted to be invaluable to her now. It helped her to assimilate and arrange the practical details of cattle-raising as put forth by the blunt Stillwell.

She split up the great stock of cattle into different herds, and when any of these were out running upon the open range, she had them closely watched. Part of the time each herd was kept in an enclosed range, fed and watered, and carefully handled by a big force of cowboys.

She employed three cowboy scouts whose sole duty was to ride the ranges searching for stray, sick, or crippled cattle or motherless calves, and to bring these in to be treated and nursed. There were two cowboys whose business was to master a pack of

Russian stag-hounds and to hunt down the coyotes, wolves, and lions that preyed upon the herds.

The better and tamer milch cows were separated from the ranging herds and kept in a pasture adjoining the dairy. All branding was done in corrals, and calves were weaned from mother-cows at the proper time to benefit both. The old method of branding and classing, that had so shocked Madeline, had been abandoned, and one had been inaugurated whereby cattle and cowboys and horses were spared brutality and injury.

Madeline established an extensive vegetable farm, and she planted orchards. The climate was superior to that of California, and, with abundant water, trees and plants and gardens flourished and bloomed in a way wonderful to behold. It was with ever-increasing pleasure that Madeline walked through acres of ground once bare, now green and bright and fragrant. There were poultry-yards and pig-pens and marshy quarters for ducks and geese. Here in the farming section of the ranch Madeline found employment for the little colony of Mexicans. Their lives had been as hard and barren as the dry valley where they had lived. But as the valley had been transformed by the soft, rich touch of water, so their lives had been transformed by help and sympathy and work. The children were wretched no more, and many that had been blind could now see, and Madeline had become to them a new and blessed virgin.

One April morning Madeline sat in her office wrestling with a problem. She had problems to solve every day. The majority of these were concerned with the management of twenty-seven incomprehensible cowboys. Stillwell faced Madeline with a smile almost as huge as his bulk.

"I don't know nothin' but cattle. Miss Majesty, it's amazin' strange what these cowboys hev come to. I never seen no cowboys like these we've got hyar now. I don't know them anymore. They dress swell an' read books, an' some of them hev actooly stopped cussin' an' drinkin'. I ain't sayin' all this is against them. Why, now, they're jest the finest bunch of cow-punchers I ever seen or dreamed of. But managin' them now is beyond me. When cowboys begin to play thet game gol-lof an' run off with French maids I reckon Bill Stillwell has got to resign."

"Stillwell! Oh, you will not leave me? What in the world would I do?" exclaimed Madeline, in great anxiety.

"Wal, I sure won't leave you, Miss Majesty. No, I never'll do thet. I'll run the cattle bizness fer you an' see after the hosses an' other stock. But I've got to hev a foreman who can handle this amazin' strange bunch of cowboys."

"You've tried half a dozen foremen. Try more until you find the man who meets your requirements," said Madeline.

Then, brightening somewhat, Stillwell turned to Madeline. "I jest hed an idee, Miss Majesty. If I can get him, Gene Stewart is the cowboy I want fer my foreman. He can manage this bunch of cow-punchers thet are drivin' me dotty. Wal, I need Gene Stewart. I need him bad. Will you let me hire him, Miss Majesty, if I can get him sobered up?"

The old cattleman ended huskily.

"Stillwell, by all means find Stewart, and do not wait to straighten him up. Bring him to the ranch," replied Madeline.

Thanking her, Stillwell led his horse away.

"Strange how he loves that cowboy!" murmured Madeline.

"Not so strange, Majesty," replied her brother. "Not when you know. Stewart has been with Stillwell on some hard trips into the desert alone. There's no middle course of feeling between men facing death in the desert. Either they hate each other or love each other. I don't know, but I imagine Stewart did something for Stillwell—saved us life, perhaps. Besides, Stewart's a lovable chap when he's going straight. I hope Stillwell brings him back. We do need him, Majesty. He's a born leader. Once I saw him ride into a bunch of Mexicans whom we suspected of rustling. It was fine to see him.

During the succeeding week Madeline discovered that a good deal of her sympathy for Stillwell in his hunt for the reckless Stewart had insensibly grown to be sympathy for the cowboy. It was rather a paradox, she thought, that opposed to the continual reports of Stewart's wildness as he caroused from town to town were the continual expressions of good will and faith and hope universally given out by those near her at the ranch. Stillwell loved the cowboy; Alfred liked and admired him, pitied him; the cowboys swore their regard for him the more he disgraced himself. The Mexicans called him El Gran Capitan.

Meanwhile Stillwell was so earnest and zealous that one not familiar with the situation would have believed he was trying to find and reclaim his own son. He made several trips to little stations in the valley, and from these he returned with a gloomy face. Madeline got the details from Alfred. Stewart was going from bad to worse— drunk, disorderly, savage, sure to land in the penitentiary. Then came a report that hurried Stillwell off to Rodeo. He returned on the third day, a crushed man. He had been so bitterly hurt that no one, not even Madeline, could get out of him what had happened. He admitted finding Stewart, failing to influence him; and when the old cattleman got so far, he turned purple in the face and talked to himself, as if dazed: "But Gene was drunk. He was drunk, or he couldn't hev treated old Bill like thet!"

Madeline was stirred with an anger toward the brutal cowboy that was as strong as her sorrow for the loyal old cattleman. And it was when Stillwell gave up that she resolved to take a hand.

Madeline stepped into a broken-down patio littered with alfalfa straw and debris, all clear in the sunlight. Upon a bench, back toward her, sat a man looking out through the rents in the broken wall. He had not heard her. The place was not quite so filthy and stifling as the passages Madeline had come through to get there. Then she saw that it had been used as a corral. A rat ran boldly across the dirt floor. The air swarmed with flies, which the man brushed at with weary hand. Madeline did not recognize Stewart. The side of his face exposed to her gaze was black, bruised, bearded. His clothes were ragged and soiled. There were bits of alfalfa in his hair. His shoulders sagged. He made a wretched and hopeless figure sitting there.

"Mr. Stewart. It is I, Miss Hammond, come to see you," she said.

He grew suddenly perfectly motionless, as if he had been changed to stone. She repeated her greeting.

His body jerked. He moved violently as if instinctively to turn and face this intruder; but a more violent movement checked him.

Madeline waited. How singular that this ruined cowboy had pride which kept him from showing his face! And was it not shame more than pride?

"Mr. Stewart, I have come to talk with you, if you will let me."

"Go away," he muttered.

"Mr. Stewart!" she began, with involuntary hauteur. But instantly she corrected herself, became deliberate and cool, for she saw that she might fail to be even heard by this man. "I have come to help you. Will you let me?"

"For God's sake! You—you—" he choked over the words. "Go away!"

"Stewart, perhaps it was for God's sake that I came," said Madeline, gently. "Surely it was for yours."

He groaned, and, staggering up to the broken wall, he leaned there with his face hidden.

"Stewart, please let me say what I have to say?"

He was silent. And she gathered courage and inspiration.

"Stillwell is deeply hurt, deeply grieved that he could not turn you back from this—this fatal course. My brother is also. They wanted to help you. I do as well. I have come, thinking somehow, I might succeed where they have failed. Stewart, we want you to come to the ranch. Stillwell needs you for his foreman. The position is open to you, and you can name your salary. Both Al and Stillwell are worried about Don Carlos, the vaqueros, and the raids down along the border. My cowboys are without a capable leader. Will you come?"

"No," he answered.

"But Stillwell wants you so badly."

199

"No."

"Stewart, I want you to come."

"No."

His replies had been hoarse, loud, furious. They disconcerted Madeline, and she paused, trying to think of a way to proceed. Stewart staggered away from the wall, and, falling upon the bench, he hid his face in his hands. All his motions, like his speech, had been violent.

"Will you please go away?" he asked.

"Stewart, certainly I cannot remain here longer if you insist upon my going. But why not listen to me when I want so much to help you? Why?"

"I'm a damned blackguard," he burst out. "But I was a gentleman once, and I'm not so low that I can stand for you seeing me here."

"When I made up my mind to help you, I made it up to see you wherever you were. Stewart, come away, come back with us to the ranch. You are in a bad condition now. Everything looks black to you. But that will pass. When you are among friends again you will get well. You will be your old self. The very fact that you were once a gentleman, that you come of good family, makes you owe so much more to yourself. Why, Stewart, think how young you are! It is a shame to waste your life. Come back with me."

"Miss Hammond, this was my last plunge," he replied, despondently. "It's too late."

"Oh no, it is not so bad as that."

"It's too late."

"At least make an effort, Stewart. Try!"

"No. There's no use. I'm done for. Please leave me—thank you for—"

"Stewart, look at me," she said.

He shuddered. She advanced and laid a hand on his bent shoulder. Under the light touch he appeared to sink.

"Look at me," she repeated.

But he could not lift his head. He was abject, crushed. He dared not show his swollen, blackened face. His fierce, cramped posture revealed more than his features might have shown; it betrayed the torturing shame of a man of pride and passion, a man who had been confronted in his degradation.

"Listen, then," went on Madeline, and her voice was unsteady. "Listen to me, Stewart. The greatest men are those who have fallen deepest into the mire, sinned most, suffered most, and then have fought their evil natures and conquered. I think you can shake off this desperate mood and be a man."

"No!" he cried.

"Listen to me again. Somehow, I know you're worthy of Stillwell's love. Will you come back with us—for his sake?"

"No. It's too late, I tell you."

"Stewart, the best thing in life is faith in human nature. I have faith in you. You are worth it."

"You can't mean it."

"I mean it with all my heart," she replied, a sudden rich warmth suffusing her body as she saw the first sign of his softening. "Will you come back—if not for your own sake or Stillwell's—then for mine?"

"What am I to such a woman as you?"

"A man in trouble, Stewart. But I have come to help you, to show my faith in you."

"If I believed that I might try," he said.

"Listen," she began, softly, hurriedly. "My word is not lightly given. Let it prove my faith in you. Look at me now and say you will come."

He heaved up his big frame as if trying to cast off a giant's burden, and then slowly he turned toward her. His face was a blotched and terrible thing. The physical brutalizing marks were there, and at that instant all that appeared human to Madeline was the dawning in dead, furnace-like eyes of a beautiful light.

"I'll come," he whispered, huskily. "Give me a few days to straighten up, then I'll come."

Zane Grey

CHAPTER 8

NELL WELLS

From *The Spirit of the Border*
(1906)

BEFORE READING *this story, be aware that it is not for the faint of heart. If violence is not your "cup of tea," you might want to skip this one though it's a powerful tale. Here is how Zane Grey presented* The Spirit of the Border *in his introduction, "The author does not intend to apologize for what many readers may call the 'brutality' of the story; but rather to explain that its wild spirit is true to the life of the Western border."*

The Spirit of the Border is Zane Grey's second novel of living on the Ohio Valley frontier where violence, often from angry Native American tribes and renegade whites, was a constant threat. The novel is a historic fiction loosely tied to the Zanes, Grey's ancestors. This story is an excerpt from that novel focusing on the massacre of Moravian missionaries and Christian converts from the Delaware Indian Tribe at Gnadenhutten, or the Village of Peace. This is a real event modified to meet Grey's imagination.

There are too many characters to describe up front. In general, there are the "good" Delaware

Indians, the "bad" Hurons, and several white missionaries.

A few characters bare special mention. Nell Wells is the niece who has travelled to the village with her uncle, a missionary. Jim Downs is a young missionary who becomes her love interest. Jim Girty is a violent white renegade raised in an Indian village. Jonathan (Jack) Zane is a frontiersman. Captain Williamson commands a unit of the Pennsylvania militia who stands by and watches the tragedy, adhering to the concept that "the only good Indian is a dead Indian." Finally, Lew Wetzel is the border's most feared Indian fighter. With the exception of the Nell, her uncle and Jim Downs, the characters are inspired by real life people.

Nell is clearly the heroine of this story, but in ways worthy of discussion. One could argue that, much like first responders today, she is a heroine because she put herself in harm's way by traveling to an Indian village that was 100 miles into the wilderness for the purpose of saving their eternal souls... which likely didn't need saving in the first place. However, for most of the novel, Nell was a woman pleading for protection from the men in the story. The one exception occurs when she steps forward to protect a child. Perhaps there is something about children that causes a woman's courage to surface?

"The prisoner suddenly raised his powerful leg, and his foot struck Girty in the pit of the stomach," *The Spirit of the Border*, A.L. Burt Company, 1906

(Illustration by J. Watson Davis)

"Whispering Winds glanced over her shoulder with a startled cry which ended in a scream. Not two yards behind her stood Jim Girty." *Spirit of the Border*, A.L. Burt Company, 1906

(Illustration by J. Watson Davis)

"Wingemund stood erect in his old, grand pose, with folded arms, while at his feet lay an Indian girl, cold as marble." *The Spirit of the Border*, A.L. Burt Company

(Illustration by J. Watson Davis)

"Nell gazed one instant into the monster's face, then like a stricken bird she fell on the grass." The Spirit of the Border, A.L. Burt Company, 1906

(Illustration by J. Watson Davis)

Zane Grey

WHEN THE FIRST RUDDY RAYS of
the rising sun crimsoned the eastern sky, Wetzel
slowly wound his way down a rugged hill far west
of Beautiful Spring. A white dog, weary and
footsore, limped by his side. Both man and beast
showed evidence of severe exertion.

The hunter stopped in a little cave under a
projecting stone, and, laying aside his rifle, began
to gather twigs and sticks. He was particular about
selecting the wood, and threw aside many pieces
which would have burned well; but when he did
kindle a flame it blazed hotly, yet made no smoke.

He sharpened a green stick, and, taking some
strips of meat from his pocket, roasted them over
the hot flame. He fed the dog first. Mose had
crouched close on the ground with his head on his
paws, and his brown eyes fastened upon the hunter.

"He had too big a start fer us," said Wetzel,
speaking as if the dog were human. It seemed that
Wetzel's words were a protest against the meaning
in those large, sad eyes.

Then the hunter put out the fire, and, searching
for a more secluded spot, finally found one on top
of the ledge, where he commanded a good view of
his surroundings. The weary dog was asleep.
Wetzel settled himself to rest, and was soon
wrapped in slumber.

About noon he awoke. He arose, stretched his
limbs, and then took an easy position on the front

of the ledge, where he could look below. Evidently the hunter was waiting for something. The dog slept on. It was the noonday hour, when the stillness of the forest almost matched that of midnight. The birds were quieter than at any other time during daylight.

Wetzel reclined there with his head against the stone, and his rifle resting across his knees.

He listened now to the sounds of the forest. The soft breeze fluttering among the leaves, the rain-call of the tree frog, the caw of crows from distant hilltops, the sweet songs of the thrush and oriole, were blended together naturally, harmoniously.

But suddenly the hunter raised his head. A note, deeper than the others, a little too strong, came from far down the shaded hollow. To Wetzel's trained ear it was a discord. He manifested no more than this attention, for the birdcall was the signal he had been awaiting. He whistled a note in answer that was as deep and clear as the one which had roused him.

Moments passed. There was no repetition of the sound. The songs of the other birds had ceased. Besides Wetzel there was another intruder in the woods.

Mose lifted his shaggy head and growled. The hunter patted the dog. In a few minutes the figure of a tall man appeared among the laurels down the slope. He stopped while gazing up at the ledge.

Then, with noiseless step, he ascended the ridge, climbed the rocky ledge, and turned the corner of the stone to face Wetzel. The newcomer was Jonathan Zane.

"Jack, I expected you afore this," was Wetzel's greeting.

"I couldn't make it sooner," answered Zane. "After we left Williamson and separated, I got turned around by a band of several hundred redskins makin' for the Village of Peace. I went back again, but couldn't find any sign of the trail we're huntin'. Then I makes for this meetin' place. I've been goin' for some ten hours, and am hungry."

"I've got some bar ready cooked," said Wetzel, handing Zane several strips of meat.

"What luck did you have?"

"I found Girty's trail, an old one, over here some eighteen or twenty miles, an' follered it until I went almost into the Delaware town.

"He's now with the renegade cutthroats and hundreds of riled Indians over there in the Village of Peace."

"I reckon you're right."

The earnest voice of the backwoodsman ceased. Both men rose and stood facing each other. Zane's bronzed face was hard and tense, expressive of an indomitable will; Wetzel's was coldly dark, with fateful resolve, as if his decree of vengeance, once given, was as immutable as destiny. The big, horny hands gripped in a viselike clasp born of fierce passion, but no word was spoken.

The two hunters turned their stern faces toward the west, and passed silently down the ridge into the depths of the forest. Darkness found them within rifle-shot of the Village of Peace. With the dog creeping between them, they crawled to a position which would, in daylight, command a view of the clearing. Then, while one stood guard, the other slept.

When morning dawned, they shifted their position to the top of a low, fern-covered cliff, from which they could see every movement in the village. All the morning they watched with that wonderful patience of men who knew how to wait. The visiting savages were quiet, the missionaries moved about in and out of the shops and cabins; the Christian Indians worked industriously in the fields, while the renegades lolled before a prominent teepee.

"This quiet looks bad," whispered Jonathan to Wetzel. No shouts were heard; not a hostile Indian was seen to move.

"They've come to a decision," whispered Jonathan, and Wetzel answered him:

"If they have, the Christians don't know it."

An hour later the deep pealing of the church bell broke the silence. The entire band of Christian Indians gathered near the large log structure, and then marched in orderly form toward the maple grove where the service was always held in pleasant weather. This movement brought the Indians within several hundred yards of the cliff where Zane and Wetzel lay concealed.

"There's Heckewelder walking with old man Wells," whispered Jonathan. "There's Young and Edwards, and, yes, there's the young missionary, brother of Joe. 'Pears to me they're foolish to hold service in the face of all those riled Injuns."

"Wuss'n foolish," answered Wetzel.

"Look! By gum! As I'm a livin' sinner there comes the whole crowd of hostile redskins. They've got their guns, and—by Gum! they're painted. Looks bad, bad! Not much friendliness about that bunch!"

"They ain't intendin' to be peaceable."

"By gum! You're right. There ain't one of them settin' down. 'Pears to me I know some of them redskins. There's Pipe, sure enough, and Kotoxen. By gum! If there ain't Shingiss; he was friendly once."

"None of them's friendly."

"Look! Lew, look! Right behind Pipe. See that long war-bonnet. As I'm a born sinner, that's your old friend, Wingenund. 'Pears to me we've rounded up all our acquaintances."

The two bordermen lay close under the tall ferns and watched the proceedings with sharp eyes. They saw the converted Indians seat themselves before the platform. The crowd of hostile Indians surrounded the glade on all sides, except one, which, singularly enough, was next to the woods.

"Look thar!" exclaimed Wetzel, under his breath. He pointed off to the right of the maple glade. Jonathan gazed in the direction indicated, and saw two savages stealthily slipping through the bushes, and behind trees. Presently these suspicious acting spies, or scouts, stopped on a little knoll perhaps a hundred yards from the glade.

Wetzel groaned.

"This ain't comfortable," growled Zane, in a low whisper. "Them red devils are up to somethin' bad. They'd better not move round over here."

The hunters, satisfied that the two isolated savages meant mischief, turned their gaze once more toward the maple grove.

"Ah! Simon you white traitor! See him, Lew, comin' with his precious gang," said Jonathan. "He's got the whole thing fixed, you can plainly see that. Bill Elliott, McKee; and who's that renegade with Jim Girty? I'll allow he must be the fellar we heard was with the Chippewas. Tough lookin' customer; a good mate fer Jim Girty! A fine lot of border-hawks!"

"Somethin' comin' off," whispered Wetzel, as Zane's low growl grew unintelligible.

Jonathan felt, rather than saw, Wetzel tremble.

"The missionaries are consultin'. Ah! there comes one! Which? I guess it's Edwards. By gum! who's that Injun stalkin' over from the hostile bunch. Big chief, whoever he is. Blest if it ain't Half King!"

The watchers saw the chief wave his arm and speak with evident arrogance to Edwards, who, however, advanced to the platform and raised his hand to address the Christians.

"Crack!"

A shot rang out from the thicket. Clutching wildly at his breast, the missionary reeled back, staggered, and fell.

"One of those skulkin' redskins has killed Edwards," said Zane. "But, no; he's not dead! He's gettin' up. Mebbe he ain't hurt bad. By gum! there's Young comin' forward. Of all the fools!"

It was indeed true that Young had faced the Indians. Half King addressed him as he had the other; but Young raised his hand and began speaking.

"Crack!"

Another shot rang out. Young threw up his hands and fell heavily. The missionaries rushed toward him. Mr. Wells ran round the group, wringing his hands as if distracted.

"He's hard hit," hissed Zane, between his teeth. "You can tell that by the way he fell."

Wetzel did not answer. He lay silent and motionless, his long body rigid, and his face like marble.

"There comes the other young fellar—Joe's brother. He'll get plugged, too," continued Zane, whispering rather to himself than to his companion. "Oh, I hoped they'd show some sense! It's noble for them to die for Christianity, but it won't do no good. By gum! Heckewelder has pulled him back. Now, that's good judgment!"

Half King stepped before the Christians and addressed them. He held in his hand a black war-club, which he wielded as he spoke.

Jonathan's attention was now directed from the maple grove to the hunter beside him. He had heard a slight metallic click, as Wetzel cocked his rifle. Then he saw the black barrel slowly rise.

"Listen, Lew. Mebbe it ain't good sense. We're after Girty, you remember; and it's a long shot from here—full three hundred yards."

"You're right, Jack, you're right," answered Wetzel, breathing hard.

"Let's wait, and see what comes off."

"Jack, I can't do it. It'll make our job harder; but I can't help it. I can put a bullet just over the Huron's left eye, an' I'm goin' to do it."

"You can't do it, Lew; you can't! It's too far for any gun. Wait! Wait!" whispered Jonathan, laying his hand on Wetzel's shoulder.

"Wait? Man, can't you see what the unnamable villain is doin'?"

"What?" asked Zane, turning his eyes again to the glade.

The converted Indians sat with bowed heads. Half King raised his war-club, and threw it on the ground in front of them.

"He's announcin' the death decree!" hissed Wetzel.

"Well! if he ain't!"

Jonathan looked at Wetzel's face. Then he rose to his knees, as had Wetzel, and tightened his belt. He knew that in another instant they would be speeding away through the forest.

"Lew, my rifle's no good fer that distance. But mebbe yours is. You ought to know. It's not sense, because there's Simon Girty, and there's Jim, the men we're after. If you can hit one, you can another. But go ahead, Lew. Plug that cowardly redskin!"

Wetzel knelt on one knee, and thrust the black rifle forward through the fern leaves. Slowly the fatal barrel rose to a level, and became as motionless as the immovable stones.

Jonathan fixed his keen gaze on the haughty countenance of Half King as he stood with folded arms and scornful mien in front of the Christians he had just condemned.

Even as the short, stinging crack of Wetzel's rifle broke the silence, Jonathan saw the fierce expression of Half King's dark face change to one of vacant wildness. His arms never relaxed from their folded position. He fell, as falls a monarch of the forest trees, a dead weight.

In the confusion the missionaries carried Young and Edwards into Mr. Wells' cabin. Nell's calm, white face showed that she had expected some such catastrophe as this, but she of all was the least excited. While Zeisberger, who was skilled in surgery, attended to the wounded men, Jim barred the heavy door, shut the rude, swinging windows, and made the cabin temporarily a refuge from prowling savages.

Outside the clamor increased. Shrill yells rent the air, long, rolling war-cries sounded above all the din. The measured stamp of moccasined feet, the rush of Indians past the cabin, the dull thud of hatchets struck hard into the trees—all attested to the excitement of the savages, and the imminence of terrible danger.

In the front room of Mr. Wells' cabin Edwards lay on a bed, his face turned to the wall, and his side exposed. There was a bloody hole in his white skin. Zeisberger was probing for the bullet. He had no instruments, save those of his own manufacture, and they were darning needles with bent points, and a long knife-blade ground thin.

"There, I have it," said Zeisberger. "Hold still, Dave. There!" As Edwards moaned Zeisberger drew forth the bloody bullet. "Jim, wash and dress this wound. It isn't bad. Dave will be all right in a couple of days. Now I'll look at George."

Zeisberger hurried into the other room. Young lay with quiet face and closed eyes, breathing faintly. Zeisberger opened the wounded man's shirt and exposed the wound, which was on the right side, rather high up. Nell, who had followed Zeisberger that she might be of some assistance if needed, saw him look at the wound and then turned a pale face away for a second. That hurried, shuddering movement of the sober, practical missionary was most significant. Then he bent over Young and inserted on of the probes into the wound. He pushed the steel an inch, two, three, four inches into Young's breast, but the latter neither moved nor moaned. Zeisberger shook his head, and finally removed the instrument. He raised the sufferer's shoulder to find the bed saturated with blood. The bullet wound extended completely through the missionary's body, and was bleeding from the back. Zeisberger folded strips of linsey cloth into small pads and bound them tightly over both apertures of the wound.

"How is he?" asked Jim, when the amateur surgeon returned to the other room, and proceeded to wash the blood from his hands.

Zeisberger shook his head gloomily.

"How is George?" whispered Edwards, who had heard Jim's question.

"Shot through the right lung. Human skill cannot aid him! Only God can save."

"Didn't I hear a third shot?" whispered Dave, gazing round with sad, questioning eyes. "Heckewelder?"

"Is safe. He has gone to see Williamson. You did hear a third shot. Half King fell dead with a bullet over his left eye. He had just folded his arms in a grand pose after his death decree to the Christians."

"A judgment of God!"

"It does seem so, but it came in the form of leaden death from Wetzel's unerring rifle. Do you hear all that yelling? Half King's death has set the Indians wild."

There was a gentle knock at the door, and then the word, "Open," in Heckewelder's voice.

Jim unbarred the door. Heckewelder came in carrying over his shoulder what apparently was a sack of meal. He was accompanied by young Christy. Heckewelder put the bag down, opened it, and lifted out a little Indian boy. The child gazed round with fearful eyes.

"Save Benny! Save Benny!" he cried, running to Nell, and she clasped him closely in her arms.

Heckewelder's face was like marble as he asked concerning Edwards' condition.

"I'm not badly off," said the missionary with a smile.

"How's George?" whispered Heckewelder.

No one answered him. Zeisberger raised his hands. All followed Heckewelder into the other room, where Young lay in the same position as when first brought in. Heckewelder stood gazing down into the wan face with its terribly significant smile.

"I brought him out here. I persuaded him to come!" whispered Heckewelder. "Oh, Almighty God!" he cried. His voice broke, and his prayer ended with the mute eloquence of clasped hands and uplifted, appealing face.

"Come out," said Zeisberger, leading him into the larger room. The others followed, and Jim closed the door.

"What's to be done?" said Zeisberger, with his practical common sense. "What did Williamson say? Tell us what you learned?"

"Wait—directly," answered Heckewelder, sitting down and covering his face with his hands. There was a long silence. At length he raised his white face and spoke calmly:

"Gentlemen, the Village of Peace is doomed. I entreated Captain Williamson to help us, but he refused. Said he dared not interfere. I prayed that he would speak at least a word to Girty, but he denied my request."

"Where are the converts?"

"Imprisoned in the church, every one of them except Benny. Mr. Christy and I hid the child in the meal sack and were thus able to get him here. We must save him."

"Save him?" asked Nell, looking from Heckewelder to the trembling Indian boy.

"Nellie, the savages have driven all our Christians into the church, and shut them up there, until Girty and his men shall give the word to complete their fiendish design. The converts asked but one favor—an hour in which to pray. It was granted. The savages intend to murder them all."

"Oh! Horrible! Monstrous!" cried Nell. "How can they be so inhuman?" She lifted Benny up in her arms. "They'll never get you, my boy. We'll save you—I'll save you!" The child moaned and clung to her neck.

"They are scouring the clearing now for Christians, and will search all the cabins. I'm positive."

"Will they come here?" asked Nell, turning her blazing eyes on Heckewelder.

"Undoubtedly. We must try to hide Benny. Let me think; where would be a good place? We'll try a dark corner of the loft."

"No, no," cried Nell.

"Put Benny in Young's bed," suggested Jim.

"No, no," cried Nell.

"Put him in a bucket and let him down in the well," whispered Edwards, who had listened intently to the conversation.

"That's a capital place," said Heckewelder. "But might he not fall out and drown?"

"Tie him in the bucket," said Jim.

"No, no, no," cried Nell.

"But Nellie, we must decide upon a hiding place, and in a hurry."

"I'll save Benny."

"You? Will you stay here to face those men? Jim Girty and Deering are searching the cabins. Could you bear it to see them? You couldn't."

"Oh! No, I believe it would kill me! That man! that beast! will he come here?" Nell grew ghastly pale, and looked as if about to faint. She shrunk in horror at the thought of again facing Girty. "For God's sake, Heckewelder, don't let him see me! Don't let him come in! Don't!"

Even as the imploring voice ceased a heavy thump sounded on the door.

"Who's there?" demanded Heckewelder.

Thump! Thump!

The heavy blows shook the cabin. The pans rattled on the shelves. No answer came from without.

"Quick! Hide Benny! It's as much as our lives are worth to have him found here," cried Heckewelder in a fierce whisper, as he darted toward the door.

"All right, all right, in a moment," he called out, fumbling over the bar.

He opened the door a moment later and when Jim Girty and Deering entered, he turned to his friends with a dread uncertainty in his haggard face.

Edwards lay on the bed with wide-open eyes staring at the intruders. Mr. Wells sat with bowed head. Zeisberger calmly whittled a stick, and Jim stood bolt upright, with a hard light in his eyes.

Nell leaned against the side of a heavy table. Wonderful was the change that had transformed her from a timid, appealing, fear-agonized girl to a woman whose only evidence of unusual excitement were the flame in her eyes and the peculiar whiteness of her face.

Benny was gone!

Heckewelder's glance returned to the visitors. He thought he had never seen such brutal, hideous men.

"Wal, I reckon a preacher ain't agoin' to lie. Hev you seen any Injun Christians round here?" asked Girty, waving a heavy sledge-hammer.

"Girty, we have hidden no Indians here," answered Heckewelder, calmly.

"Wal, we'll hev a look, anyway," answered the renegade.

Girty surveyed the room with wolfish eyes. Deering was so drunk that he staggered. Both men, in fact, reeked with the vile fumes of rum. Without another word they proceeded to examine the room, by looking into every box, behind a stone oven, and in the cupboard. They drew the bedclothes from the bed, and with a kick demolished a pile of stove wood. Then the ruffians passed into the other apartments, where they could be heard making thorough search. At length both returned to the large room, when Girty directed Deering to climb a ladder leading to the loft, but because Deering was too much under the influence of liquor to do so, he had to go himself. He rummaged around up there for a few minutes, and then came down.

"Wal, I reckon you wasn't lyin' about it," said Girty, with his ghastly leer.

He and his companion started to go out. Deering had stood with bloodshot eyes fixed on Nell while Girty searched the loft, and as they passed the girl on their way to the open air, the renegade looked at Girty as he motioned with his head toward her. His besotted face expressed some terrible meaning.

Girty had looked at Nell when he first entered, but had not glanced twice at her. As he turned now, before going out of the door, he fixed on her his baleful glance. His aspect was fuller of meaning than could have been any words. A horrible power, of which he was boastfully conscious, shone from his little, pointed eyes. His mere presence was deadly. Plainly as if he had spoken was the significance of his long gaze. Anyone could have translated that look.

Once before Nell had faced it, and fainted when its dread meaning grew clear to her. But now she returned his gaze with one in which flashed lightning scorn, and repulsion, in which glowed a wonderful defiance.

The cruel face of this man, the boastful barbarity of his manner, the long, dark, bloody history which his presence recalled, was, indeed, terrifying without the added horror of his intent toward her, but now the self-forgetfulness of a true woman sustained her.

Girty and Deering backed out of the door. Heckewelder closed it, and dropped the bar in place.

Nell fell over the table with a long, low gasp. Then with one hand she lifted her skirt. Benny walked from under it. His big eyes were bright. The young woman clasped him again in her arms. Then she released him, and, laboring under intense excitement, ran to the window.

"There he goes! Oh, the horrible beast! If I only had a gun and could shoot! Oh, if only I were a man! I'd kill him. To think of poor Kate! Ah! he intends the same for me!"

Suddenly she fell upon the floor in a faint. Mr. Wells and Jim lifted her on the bed beside Edwards, where they endeavored to revive her. It was some moments before she opened her eyes.

Jim sat holding Nell's hand. Mr. Wells again bowed his head. Zeisberger continued to whittle a stick, and Heckewelder paced the floor. Christy stood by with every evidence of sympathy for this distracted group. Outside the clamor increased.

"Just listen!" cried Heckewelder. "Did you ever hear the like? All drunk, crazy, fiendish! They drank every drop of liquor the French traders had. Curses on the vagabond dealers! Rum has made these renegades and savages wild. Oh! my poor, innocent Christians!"

Heckewelder leaned his head against the mantle-shelf. He had broken down at last. Racking sobs shook his frame.

"Are you all right again?" asked Jim of Nell.

"Yes."

"I am going out, first to see Williamson, and then the Christians," he said, rising very pale, but calm.

"Don't go!" cried Heckewelder. "I have tried everything. It was all of no use."

"I will go," answered Jim.

"Yes, Jim, go," whispered Nell, looking up into his eyes. It was an earnest gaze in which a faint hope shone.

Jim unbarred the door and went out.

"Wait, I'll go along," cried Zeisberger, suddenly dropping his knife and stick.

As the two men went out a fearful spectacle met their eyes. The clearing was alive with Indians. But such Indians! They were painted demons, maddened by rum. Yesterday they had been silent; if they moved at all it had been with deliberation and dignity. To-day they were a yelling, running, blood-seeking mob.

"Awful! Did you ever see human beings like these?" asked Zeisberger.

"No, no!"

"I saw such a frenzy once before, but, of course, only in a small band of savages. Many times, have I seen Indians preparing for the war-path, in search of both white men and redskins. They were fierce then, but nothing like this. Every one of these frenzied fiends is honest. Think of that! Every man feels it his duty to murder these Christians. Girty has led up to this by cunning, and now the time is come to let them loose."

"It means death for all."

"I have given up any thought of escaping," said Zeisberger, with the calmness that had characterized his manner since he returned to the village. "I shall try to get into the church."

"I'll join you there as soon as I see Williamson."

Jim walked rapidly across the clearing to the cabin where Captain Williamson had quarters. The frontiersmen stood in groups, watching the savages with an interest which showed little or no concern.

"I want to see Captain Williamson," said Jim to a frontiersman on guard at the cabin door.

"Wal, he's inside," drawled the man.

Jim thought the voice familiar, and he turned sharply to see the sun-burnt features of Jeff Lynn, the old riverman who had taken Mr. Wells' party to Fort Henry.

"Why, Lynn! I'm glad to see you," exclaimed Jim.

"I'm in a hurry. Do you think Captain Williamson will stand still and let all this go on?"

"I'm afeerd so."

Evidently the captain heard the conversation, for he appeared at the cabin door, smoking a long pipe.

"Captain Williamson, I have come to entreat you to save the Christians from this impending massacre."

"I can't do nuthin'," answered Williamson, removing his pipe to puff forth a great cloud of smoke.

My God!" cried Jim, voicing the passion which consumed him. "You are white men, yet you will stand by and see these innocent people murdered! Man, where's your humanity? Your manhood? These converted Indians are savages no longer; they are Christians. Their children are as good, pure, innocent as your own. Can you remain idle and see these little ones murdered?"

Williamson made no answer, the men who had crowded round were equally silent. Not one lowered his head. Many looked at the impassioned missionary; others gazed at the savages who were circling around the trees brandishing their weapons. If any pitied the unfortunate Christians, none showed it. They were indifferent, with the indifference of men hardened to cruel scenes.

Jim understood, at last, as he turned from face to face to find everywhere that same imperturbability. These bordermen were like Wetzel and Jonathan Zane. The only good Indian was a dead Indian. Years of war and bloodshed, of merciless cruelty at the hands of redmen, of the hard, border life had rendered these frontiersmen incapable of compassion for any savage.

Jim no longer restrained himself.

"Bordermen you may be, but from my standpoint, from any man's, from God's, you are a lot of coldly indifferent cowards!" exclaimed Jim, with white, quivering lips. "I understand now. Few of you will risk anything for Indians. You will not believe a savage can be a Christian. You don't care if they are all murdered. Any man among you—any man, I say—would step out before those howling fiends and boldly demand that there be no bloodshed. A courageous leader with a band of determined followers could avert this tragedy. You might readily intimidate yonder horde of drunken demons. Captain Williamson, I am only a minister, far removed from a man of war and leader, as you claim to be, but, sir, I curse you as a miserable coward. If I ever get back to civilization, I'll brand this inhuman coldness of yours, as the most infamous and dastardly cowardice that ever disgraced a white man. You are worse than Girty!"

Jim hardly knew which way to turn. He would make one more effort. He crossed the clearing to where the renegades' teepee stood. Simon Girty stood, his hard, keen, roving eyes on the scene.

There was a difference in his aspect, a wilder look than the others wore, as if the man had suddenly awakened to the fury of his Indians. Nevertheless, the young man went straight toward him.

"Girty, I come——"

"Git out! You meddlin' preacher!" yelled the renegade, shaking his fist at Jim.

Simon Girty was drunk.

Jim turned from the white fiends. He knew his life to them was not worth a pinch of powder.

"Lost! Lost! All lost!" he exclaimed in despair.

As he went toward the church, he saw hundreds of savages bounding over the grass, brandishing weapons and whooping fiendishly. They were concentrating around Girty's teepee, where already a great throng had congregated. Of all the Indians to be seen not one walked. They leaped by Jim, and ran over the grass nimble as deer.

He saw the eager fire in their dusky eyes, and the cruelly clenched teeth like those of wolves when they snarl. He felt the hissing breath of many savages as they raced by him. More than one whirled a tomahawk close to Jim's head, and uttered horrible yells in his ear. They were like tigers lusting for blood.

Jim hurried to the church. Not an Indian was visible near the log structure. Even the savage guards had gone. He entered the open door to be instantly struck with reverence and awe.

The Christians were singing.

Miserable and full of sickening dread though Jim was, he could not but realize that the scene before him was one of extraordinary beauty and pathos. The doomed Indians lifted up their voices in song. Never had they sung so feelingly, so harmoniously.

When the song ended Zeisberger, who stood upon a platform, opened his Bible and read:

"In a little wrath I hid my face from thee for a moment, but with everlasting kindness will I have mercy on thee, saith the Lord, thy Redeemer."

In a voice low and tremulous the venerable missionary began his sermon.

The shadow of death hovered over these Christian martyrs; it was reflected in their somber eyes, yet not one was sullen or sad. The children who were too young to understand, but instinctively feeling the tragedy soon to be enacted there, cowered close to their mothers.

Zeisberger preached a touching and impressive, though short, sermon. At its conclusion the whole congregation rose and surrounded the missionary. The men shook his hands, the women kissed them, the children clung to his legs. It was a wonderful manifestation of affection.

Suddenly Glickhican, the old Delaware chief, stepped on the platform, raised his hand and shouted one Indian word.

A long, low wail went up from the children and youths; the women slowly, meekly bowed their heads. The men, due to the stoicism of their nature and the Christianity they had learned, stood proudly erect awaiting the death that had been decreed.

Glickhican pulled the bell rope.

A deep, mellow tone pealed out.

The sound transfixed all the Christians. No one moved.

Glickhican had given the signal which told the murderers the Christians were ready.

"Come, man, my God! We can't stay here!" cried Jim to Zeisberger.

As they went out both men turned to look their last on the martyrs. The death knell which had rung in the ears of the Christians, was to them the voice of God. Stern, dark visages of men and the sweet, submissive faces of women were uplifted with rapt attention. A light seemed to shine from these faces as if the contemplation of God had illumined them.

As Zeisberger and Jim left the church and hurried toward the cabins, they saw the crowd of savages in a black mass round Girty's teepee. The yelling and leaping had ceased.

Heckewelder opened the door. Evidently, he had watched for them.

"Jim! Jim!" cried Nell, when he entered the cabin. "Oh-h! I was afraid. Oh! I am glad you're back safe. See, this noble Indian has come to help us."

Wingenund stood calm and erect by the door.

"Chief, what will you do?"

"Wingenund will show you the way to the big river," answered the chieftain, in his deep bass.

"Run away? No, never! That would be cowardly. Heckewelder, you would not go? Nor you, Zeisberger? We may yet be of use, we may yet save some of the Christians."

"Save the yellow-hair," sternly said Wingenund.

"Oh, Jim, you don't understand. The chief has come to warn me of Girty. He intends to take me. Did you not see the meaning in his eyes to-day? How they scorched me! Ho! Jim, take me away! Save me! Do not leave me here to that horrible fate? Oh! Jim, take me away!"

"Nell, I will take you," cried Jim, grasping her hands.

"Hurry! There's a blanket full of things I packed for you," said Heckewelder. "Lose no time. Ah! hear that! My Heavens! what a yell!" Heckewelder rushed to the door and looked out. "There they go, a black mob of imps; a pack of hungry wolves! Jim Girty is in the lead. How he leaps! How he waves his sledge! He leads the savages toward the church. Oh! it's the end!"

"Benny? Where's Benny?" cried Jim, hurriedly lacing the hunting coat he had flung about him.

"Benny's safe. I've hidden him. I'll get him away from here," answered young Christy. "Go! Now's your time. Godspeed you!"

"I'm ready," declared Mr. Wells. "I—have—finished!"

"There goes Wingenund! He's running. Follow him, quick! Good-by! Good-by! God be with you!" cried Heckewelder.

"Good-by! Good-by!"

Jim hurried Nell toward the bushes where Wingenund's tall form could dimly be seen. Mr. Wells followed them.

Never speaking, never looking back, the guide hurried eastward with long strides. His followers were almost forced to run in order to keep him in sight. He had waited at the edge of the clearing for them, and, relieving Jim of the heavy pack, which he swung slightly over his shoulder, he set a pace that was most difficult to maintain. The young missionary half led, half carried Nell over the stones and rough places. Mr. Wells labored in the rear.

Wingenund halted for them at the height of a ridge where the forest was open.

"Ugh!" exclaimed the chieftain, as they finished the ascent. He stretched a long arm toward the sun; his falcon eye gleamed.

Far in the west a great black and yellow cloud of smoke rolled heavenward. It seemed to rise from out the forest, and to hang low over the trees; then it soared aloft and grew thinner until it lost its distinct line far in the clouds. The setting sun stood yet an hour high over a distant hill, and burned dark red through the great pall of smoke.

"Is it a forest fire?" asked Nell, fearfully.

"Fire, of course, but——-" Jim did not voice his fear; he looked closely at Wingenund.

The chieftain stood silent a moment as was his wont when addressed. The dull glow of the sun was reflected in the dark eyes that gazed far away over forest and field.

"Fire," said Wingenund, and it seemed that as he spoke a sterner shadow flitted across his bronzed face. "The sun sets to-night over the ashes of the Village of Peace."

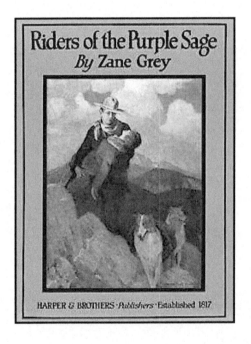

CHAPTER 9

JANE WITHERSTEEN

From *Riders of the Purple Sage* (1912)

Riders of the Purple Sage *was chosen by the Library of Congress as "one of the books that shaped America." The novel tells the story of a young woman, Jane Withersteen, who has inherited a huge ranch in a remote Mormon community. Immoral Bishop Dyer and equally evil churchman Elder Tull work together in hopes of forcing Jane into a polygamist marriage and gaining control of her ranch.*

Though Jane is one of Zane Grey's best-known characters, there are Grey fans who cringe at calling her a heroine. One peer commented, "Why, oh, why, would someone as strong as Jane W. allow herself to be stripped of her property and bankrupted in that way," Another concern is why she had to hire a gunman to protect her.

In today's world of increasingly stronger, more liberated women, I can see why Jane's behavior would meet with some condemnation. However, like Jane, I'm a member of the Church of Jesus Christ of Latter-day Saints and have a different perspective.

Truthfully, Grey missed a powerful opportunity, likely due to his lack of understand regarding the workings of the LDS faith. Jane would have been terrified if her bishop had ordered a "church court" to consider disfellowshipping or excommunicating her for her behavior. For a member of the faith, such an action would threaten his or her eternal life, not just her days here on earth. To me, Jane showed the courage of her convictions in her decisions and, in the process, was more heroic than most of Grey's protagonists. As an educated woman, she assuredly would have read the Bible and found inspiration in Luke 20: 46:

> *"Beware of the teachers of the law. They like to walk around in flowing robes and love to be greeted with respect in the marketplaces and have the most important seats in the synagogues and the places of honor at banquets. They devour widows' houses and for a show make lengthy prayers. These men will be punished most severely."*

It is important to understand that the evil ways of Bishop Dyer and Elder Tull are absolutely NOT representative of the Latter-day Saint faith. Members would be appalled with what they would consider "unrighteous dominion."

Jane is a unique heroine who quietly fights abuse of power by churchmen who wield their authority to dominate a good woman. In doing so, her heroic character outshines the villains as she lives her religious teachings in the face of oppression. In today's world where so many women choose to stay in abusive relationships, Jane's choice reflects the uncredited saying:

"Knowing when to walk away, is wisdom. Being able to, is courage. Walking away with your head held high is dignity."

In the following story, Jane experiences spiritual pressure from those of her faith, while displaying the kind of Christian charity needed more in the world today.

Riders of the Purple Sage *poses the question, "Is the hero always the one wielding the biggest gun?"*

Sisters of the Sage

"Lassiter, will you be my rider?" Jane asked him.

"I reckon so," he had replied.

From that hour, it seemed, Lassiter was always in the saddle, riding early and late, and coincident with his part in Jane's affairs the days assumed their old tranquility. Her intelligence told her this was only the lull before the storm, but her faith would not have it so.

She resumed her visits to the village, and upon one of these she encountered Tull. He greeted her as he had before any trouble came between them, and she, responsive to peace if not quick to forget, met him halfway with manner almost cheerful. He regretted the loss of her cattle; he assured her that the vigilantes which had been organized would soon rout the rustlers; when that had been accomplished her riders would likely return to her.

"You've done a headstrong thing to hire this man Lassiter," Tull went on, severely. "He came to Cottonwoods with evil intent."

"I had to have somebody. And perhaps making him my rider may turn out best in the end for the Mormons of Cottonwoods."

"You mean to stay his hand?"

"I do—if I can."

"A woman like you can do anything with a man. That would be well, and would atone in some measure for the errors you have made."

He bowed and passed on. Jane resumed her walk with conflicting thoughts. She resented Elder Tull's cold, impassive manner that looked down upon her as one who had incurred his just displeasure. Otherwise he would have been the same calm, dark-browed, impenetrable man she had known for ten years. He stood out now a strange, secretive man.

She would have thought better of him if he had picked up the threads of their quarrel where they had parted. Was Tull what he appeared to be? The question flung itself in-voluntarily over Jane Withersteen's inhibitive habit of faith without question. And she refused to answer it. Tull could not fight in the open. Lassiter had said, that her Elder shirked fight and worked in the dark. Just now in this meeting Tull had ignored the fact that he had sued, exhorted, demanded that she marry him. His manner was that of the minister who had been outraged, but who overlooked the frailties of a woman. Beyond question he seemed unutterably aloof from all knowledge of pressure being brought to bear upon her, absolutely guiltless of any connection with secret power over riders, with night journeys, with rustlers and stampedes of cattle. And that convinced her again of unjust suspicions. But it was convincement through an obstinate faith. She shuddered as she accepted it, and that shudder was the nucleus of a terrible revolt.

Jane turned into one of the wide lanes leading from the main street and entered a huge, shady yard. Here were sweet-smelling clover, alfalfa, flowers, and vegetables, all growing in happy confusion. And like these fresh green things were the dozens of babies, tots, toddlers, noisy urchins, laughing girls, a whole multitude of children of one family. Collier Brandt, the father of all this numerous progeny, was a Mormon with four wives.

In the shade of a wide, low, vine-roofed porch Jane found Brandt's wives entertaining Bishop Dyer. They were motherly women, of comparatively similar ages, and plain-featured, and just at this moment anything but grave. The Bishop was rather tall, of stout build, with iron-gray hair and beard, and eyes of light blue. They were merry now; but Jane had seen them when they werc not, and then she feared him as she had feared her father.

The women flocked around her in welcome.

"Daughter of Withersteen," said the Bishop, gaily, as he took her hand, "you have not been prodigal of your gracious self of late. A Sabbath without you at service! I shall reprove Elder Tull."

"Bishop, the guilt is mine. I'll come to you and confess," Jane replied, lightly; but she felt the undercurrcnt of her words.

"Mormon love-making!" exclaimed the Bishop, rubbing his hands. "Tull keeps you all to himself."

"No. He is not courting me."

"What? The laggard! If he does not make haste, I'll go a-courting myself up to Withersteen House."

There was laughter and further bantering by the Bishop, and then mild talk of village affairs, after which he took his leave, and Jane was left with her friend, Mary Brandt.

"Jane, you're not yourself. Are you sad about the rustling of the cattle? But you have so many, you are so rich."

Then Jane confided in her, telling much, yet holding back her doubts of fear.

"Oh, why don't you marry Tull and be one of us?

"But, Mary, I don't love Tull," said Jane, stubbornly.

"I don't blame you for that. But, Jane Withersteen, you've got to choose between the love of man and love of God. Often, we Mormon women have to do that. It's not easy. The kind of happiness you want I wanted once. I never got it, nor will you, unless you throw away your soul. Some dreadful thing will come of it. Marry Tull. It's your duty as a Mormon. You'll feel no rapture as his wife—but think of Heaven! Mormon women don't marry for what they expect on earth. Take up the cross, Jane. Remember your father found Amber Spring, built these old houses, brought Mormons here, and fathered them. You are the daughter of Withersteen!"

Jane left Mary Brandt and went to call upon other friends. They received her with the same glad welcome as had Mary, lavished upon her the pent-up affection of Mormon women, and let her go with her ears ringing of Tull, Lassiter, of duty to God and glory in Heaven.

"Verily," murmured Jane, "I don't know myself when, through all this, I remain unchanged—nay, more fixed of purpose."

She returned to the main street and bent her thoughtful steps toward the center of the village. A string of wagons drawn by oxen was lumbering along. These "sage-freighters," as they were called, hauled grain and flour and merchandise from Sterling, and Jane laughed suddenly in the midst of her humility at the thought that they were her property, as was one of the three stores for which they freighted goods. The water that flowed along the path at her feet, and turned into each cottage-yard to nourish garden and orchard, also was hers, no less her private property because she chose to give it free. Yet in this village of Cottonwoods, which her father had founded and which she maintained she was not her own mistress; she was not able to abide by her own choice of a husband. She was the daughter of Withersteen.

As she went on down the street past the stores with their rude platform entrances, and the saloons where tired horses stood with bridles dragging, she was again assured of what was the bread and wine of life to her—that she was loved. Dirty boys playing in the ditch, clerks, teamsters, riders, loungers on the corners, ranchers on dusty horses, little girls running errands, and women hurrying to the stores all looked up at her coming with glad eyes.

Jane's various calls and wandering steps at length led her to the Gentile quarter of the village. This was at the extreme southern end, and here some thirty Gentile families lived in huts and shacks and log-cabins and several dilapidated cottages. The fortunes of these inhabitants of Cottonwoods could be read in their abodes. Water they had in abundance, and therefore grass and fruit-trees and patches of alfalfa and vegetable gardens. Some of the men and boys had a few stray cattle, others obtained such intermittent employment as the Mormons reluctantly tendered them. But none of the families was prosperous, many were very poor, and some lived only by Jane Withersteen's beneficence.

As it made Jane happy to go among her own people, so it saddened her to come in contact with these Gentiles. Yet that was not because she was unwelcome; here she was gratefully received by the women, passionately by the children. But poverty and idleness, with their attendant wretchedness and sorrow, always hurt her. That she could alleviate this distress more now than ever before proved the adage that it was an ill wind that blew nobody good.

Down the lane, Jane came upon a gentile named Carson who had been a rider for her ranch for years, but recently resigned.

"It won't do," said one Carson. "We've had our warning. Can we risk having our homes burned in our absence?"

Jane felt the stretching and chilling of the skin of her face as the blood left it.

"Carson, you and the others rent these houses?" she asked.

"You ought to know, Miss Withersteen. Some of them are yours."

"I know?... Carson, I never in my life took a day's labor for rent or a yearling calf or a bunch of grass, let alone gold."

"Bivens, your store-keeper, sees to that."

"Look here, Carson," went on Jane, hurriedly, and now her cheeks were burning. "You and Black and Willet pack your goods and move your families up to my cabins in the grove. They're far more comfortable than these. Then go to work for me. And if aught happens to you there I'll give you money—gold enough to leave Utah!"

The man choked and stammered, and then, as tears welled into his eyes, he found the use of his tongue and cursed. No gentle speech could ever have equaled that curse in eloquent expression of what he felt for Jane Withersteen. How strangely his look and tone reminded her of Lassiter!

"No, it won't do," he said, when he had somewhat recovered himself. "Miss Withersteen, there are things that you don't know, and there's not a soul among us who can tell you."

"I seem to be learning many things, Carson. Well, then, will you let me aid you—say till better times?"

"Yes, I will," he replied, with his face lighting up. "I see what it means to you, and you know what it means to me. Thank you! And if better times ever come, I'll be only too happy to work for you."

"Better times will come. I trust God and have faith in man. Good day, Carson."

The lane opened out upon the sage-enclosed alfalfa fields, and the last habitation, at the end of that lane of hovels, was the meanest. Formerly it had been a shed; now it was a home. The broad leaves of a wide-spreading cottonwood sheltered the sunken roof of weathered boards. Like an Indian hut, it had one floor. Round about it were a few scanty rows of vegetables, such as the hand of a weak woman had time and strength to cultivate. This little dwelling-place was just outside the village limits, and the widow who lived there had to carry her water from the nearest irrigation ditch. As Jane Withersteen entered the unfenced yard a child saw her, shrieked with joy, and came tearing toward her with curls flying. This child was a little girl of four called Fay. Her name suited her, for she was an elf, a sprite, a creature so fairy-like and beautiful that she seemed unearthly.

"Muvver sended for oo," cried Fay, as Jane kissed her, "an' oo never come."

"I didn't know, Fay; but I've come now."

Fay was a child of outdoors, of the garden and ditch and field, and she was dirty and ragged. But rags and dirt did not hide her beauty. The one thin little bedraggled garment she wore half covered her fine, slim body. Red as cherries were her cheeks and lips; her eyes were violet blue, and the crown of her childish loveliness was the curling golden hair. All the children of Cottonwoods were Jane Withersteen's friends, she loved them all. But Fay was dearest to her. Fay had few playmates, for among the Gentile children there were none near her age, and the Mormon children were forbidden to play with her. So, she was a shy, wild, lonely child.

"Muvver's sick," said Fay, leading Jane toward the door of the hut.

Jane went in. There was only one room, rather dark and bare, but it was clean and neat. A woman lay upon a bed.

"Mrs. Larkin, how are you?" asked Jane, anxiously.

"I've been pretty bad for a week, but I'm better now."

"You haven't been here all alone—with no one to wait on you?"

"Oh no! My women neighbors are kind. They take turns coming in."

"Did you send for me?"

"Yes, several times."

"But I had no word—no messages ever got to me."

"I sent the boys, and they left word with your women that I was ill and would you please come."

A sudden deadly sickness seized Jane. She fought the weakness, as she fought to be above suspicious thoughts, and it passed, leaving her conscious of her utter impotence. That, too, passed as her spirit rebounded. But she had again caught a glimpse of dark underhand domination, running its secret lines this time into her own household. Like a spider in the blackness of night an unseen hand had begun to run these dark lines, to turn and twist them about her life, to plait and weave a web. Jane Withersteen knew it now, and in the realization further coolness and sureness came to her, and the fighting courage of her ancestors.

"Mrs. Larkin, you're better, and I'm so glad," said Jane. "But may I not do something for you—a turn at nursing, or send you things, or take care of Fay?"

"You're so good. Since my husband's been gone what would have become of Fay and me but for you? It was about Fay that I wanted to speak to you. This time I thought surely, I'd die, and I was worried about Fay. Well, I'll be around all right shortly, but my strength's gone and I won't live long. So, I may as well speak now. You remember asking me to let you take Fay and bring her up as your daughter?"

"Indeed yes, I remember. I'll be happy to have her. But I hope the day——"

"Never mind that. The day'll come—sooner or later. I refused your offer, and now I'll tell you why."

"I know why," interposed Jane. "It's because you don't want her brought up as a Mormon."

"No, it wasn't altogether that." Mrs. Larkin raised her thin hand and laid it appealingly on Jane's. "I don't like to tell you. But—it's this. I told all my friends what you wanted. They know you, care for you, and they said for me to trust Fay to you. Women will talk, you know. It got to the ears of Mormons—gossip of your love for Fay and your wanting her. And it came straight back to me, in jealousy, perhaps, that you wouldn't take Fay as much for love of her as because of your religious duty to bring up another girl for some Mormon to marry."

"That's a damnable lie!" cried Jane Withersteen.

"It was what made me hesitate," went on Mrs. Larkin, "but I never believed it at heart. And now I guess I'll let you——"

"Wait! Mrs. Larkin. Believe me. I love little Fay. If I had her near me, I'd grow to worship her.

255

When I asked for her, I thought only of that love....
Let me prove this. You and Fay come to live with
me. I've such a big house, and I'm so lonely. I'll help
nurse you, take care of you. When you're better you
can work for me. I'll keep little Fay and bring her
up—without Mormon teaching. When she's grown,
if she should want to leave me, I'll send her, and not
empty-handed, back to Illinois where you came
from."

"I knew it was a lie," replied the mother, and
she sank back upon her pillow with something of
peace in her white, worn face. "Jane Withersteen,
may Heaven bless you! I've been deeply grateful to
you. But because you're a Mormon I never felt close
to you till now. I don't know much about religion as
religion, but your God and my God are the same."

Zane Grey

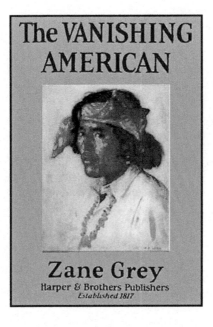

CHAPTER 10
MARIAN WARNER
From *The Vanishing American* (1925)

Marian Warner is the heroine in The Vanishing American, *one of Zane Grey's most controversial novel. This indictment of the missionary education system on the Navajo Reservation is based on information gathered by the author during his many visits to the area. A passage from "American Indian Education, A History" perhaps best summarizes the reasons for the controversy:*

The publishers [of The Vanishing American] delayed the book version because religious groups were offended by its portrayal of missionaries raping Indian girls and stealing Indian land. Grey was forced to kill off his Navajo hero rather than have him marry the white heroine and to tone down his indictment of missionaries. In the movie version the missionaries were eliminated. Even into the 1950s twenty-six states had ant miscegenation laws [which made interracial marriage illegal]. (John Allen Rayhner and Jeanne Eder, American Indian Education: A History, University of Oklahoma Press, Norman 2004, p. 205)

The story we are sharing doesn't need an introduction other than explaining that it involves a discussion between Marian Warner, the blonde heroine of the novel, and Mrs. Withers. Withers is based on Zane Grey's friend, Louisa Wetherill, a real-life heroine married to the famous Indian trader, John Wetherill. John is also briefly featured in the story. The story begins just after Marian arrives at the reservation in response to a letter from her lover, a Navajo named Nophaie. The passages do a great job of summarizing the themes of the novel.

Before moving on to the story, we need to address the issue of heroism, and I'll let you decide. It's the 1920s and Marian chooses to leave city life on the East Coast and travel to the Navajo reservation, one of the poorest places in America. Her reason is that she wants to pursue an interracial relationship with a Navajo man during a time when society condemned such love affairs. Is that brave or is it foolish?

Zane Grey

Sisters of the Sage

CLOSE AT HAND, Kaidab trading post showed striking aspects of life and activity. Marian looked and looked, with mounting delight and wonder.

First there were a number of the shaggy Indian ponies, unhaltered, standing with uplifted heads, and black rolling eyes askance on the mail carrier's car. Several were without saddles, having blankets tied on their backs; one was of a cream color almost pink, with strange light eyes and wonderful long mane and tail; most of them were a reddish bay in color; and there was a fiery little black that took Marian's eye.

Huge bags of burlap containing wool were being packed into a wagon by Indian freighters. And Indians were lounging around, leaning against the stone wall of the trading post. The look of them somehow satisfied Marian. Raven-black hair, impassive faces of bronze, eyes of night, lean and erect figures clad in velvet and corduroy, with glints of silver and bead ornament—these circumstances of appearance came somewhere near fitting Marian's rather sentimental anticipations.

Before the open front of one building, evidently a storehouse, other Indians were packing wool in long sacks, a laborsome task, to judge from their efforts to hold the sack erect and stamp down the wool. The whole interior of this open house appeared hung and littered with harness, rope, piles of white sacks, piles of wool and skins. The odor of

263

sheep struck Marian rather disagreeably. The sun was hot, and fell glaringly upon the red blankets. Flies buzzed everywhere. And at least a dozen lean, wild- looking and inquisitive-eyed dogs sniffed around Marian. Not one of them wagged its tail. White men in shirt sleeves, with sweaty faces and hands begrimed, were working over a motor-car as dilapidated as the mail carriers.

Two Indian women, laden with bundles, came out of the open door of the trading post. The older woman was fat and pleasant-faced. She wore loose flowing garments, gaudy in color, and silver necklaces, and upon her back she carried a large bundle or box. When she passed, Marian caught a glimpse of a dark little baby face peering out of a hole in that box. The younger female was probably a daughter, and she was not uncomely in appearance. Something piquant and bright haunted her smooth dark face. She was slender. She had little feet incased in brown moccasins. She wore what Marian thought was velveteen, and her silver ornaments were studded with crude blue stones. She glanced shyly at Marian.

Then an Indian came riding up to dismount near Marian. He was old. His lean face was a mass of wrinkles, and there was iron gray in his hair. He wore a thin cotton shirt and overalls— white man's apparel much the worse for wear. Behind his saddle hung a long bundle, a goatskin rolled with the fur inside. This he untied and carried into the trading post.

More Indians came riding in; one of the ponies began to rear and snort and kick; the dogs barked; whisks of warm and odorous wind stirred the dust; the smell of the sheep wool grew stronger; low guttural voices of Indians mingled with the sharper, higher notes of white men.

A sturdily built, keen-eyed man stalked out of the post, with a hand on the Indian mail carrier's shoulder. He wore a vest over a flannel shirt, but no coat or hat. His boots were rough and dusty.

"Take her bags in," he said to the Indian.

Then, at his near approach, Marian felt herself scanned by a gaze at once piercing and kindly.

"Glad to welcome you, Miss Warner," he said. "Been expecting you for two hours. I'm John Withers."

Marian offered her hand. "Expecting me?" she queried, curiously.

"News travels fast in this country," he replied, with a smile. "An Indian rode in two hours ago with the news you were coming."

"But my name?" asked Marian, still curious.

"Mrs. Withers told me that and what you looked like. She'll shore be glad to see you. Come, we'll go in."

Marian followed him into the yard beside the trading post, where somewhat in the background stood a low, squat, picturesque stone house with roof of red earth. Her curiosity had developed into wonder. She tingled a little at an implication that followed one of her conjectures. How could Mrs. Withers know what she looked like?

Withers ushered her into a wonderful room that seemed to flash Indian color and design at her. Blankets on floor and couch, baskets on mantel and wall, and a strange painted frieze of Indian figures, crude, elemental, striking—these lent the room its atmosphere. A bright fire blazed in the open stone fireplace. Books and comforts were not lacking. This room opened into a long dining-room, with the same ornamental Indian effects. And from it ran a hallway remarkable for its length and variety and color of its decorations.

Marian's quick eyes had only time for one look when a woman of slight stature and remarkable face entered.

"Welcome to Kaidab, Miss Warner," she said, warmly, with extended hands. "We're happy to meet you. We hope you will stay long."

"Thank you, Mrs. Withers. You're very kind. I—I am very glad to get here," replied Marian, just a little confused and nervous.

"You've had a long, cold ride. And you're red with dust. Oh, I know that ride. I took it first twenty-five years ago, on horseback."

"Yes, it was hard. And cold—I nearly froze. But, oh, it was wonderful!"

Withers laughed his pleasure at her words. "Why, that's no ride. You're just on the edge of real wild country. We're going to show you."

"John, put Miss Warner's bags in the second room. And send some hot water. After she's comfortable and rested we can talk."

Marian found the room quaint and strange as the others. It had a clean, earthy smell. The walls appeared to be red cement—adobe, Marian supposed—and they were cold.

While washing and changing her dusty clothes she pondered over her singular impressions of Mrs. Withers. She was no ordinary woman. For some reason not apparent to Marian her hostess had a strong personal regard for her. Marian had intuitively felt this. Besides she must have been a woman used to welcoming strangers to this wild frontier. Marian sensed something of the power she had felt in women of high position, as they met their guests; only in the case of Mrs. Withers it was a simplicity of power, a strange, unconscious dignity, spiritual rather than material. But Marian lost no time in making herself comfortable or conjecturing about Mrs. Withers. She felt drawn to this woman. She divined news, strange portents, unknown possibilities, all of which hurried her back to the living room. Mrs. Withers was there, waiting for her.

"How sweet and fair you are!" exclaimed Mrs. Withers, with an admiring glance at Marian's face.

"We don't see your kind out here. The desert is hard on blondes."

"So, I imagine," replied Marian. "I'll not long remain 'Benow di cleash!'... Is that pronounced correctly?"

Mrs. Withers laughed. "Well, I understand you. But you must say it this way... 'Benow di cleash!'"

Her voice had some strange, low, liquid quality utterly new to Marian.

"Mrs. Withers, you know where I got that name," asserted Marian.

"Yes, I'm happy to tell you I do," she rejoined, earnestly. Marian slowly answered to the instinct of the moment. Her hands went out to meet those offered by Mrs. Withers, and she gazed down into the strange strong face with its shadows of sorrow and thought, its eyes of penetrating and mystic power.

"Let us sit down," continued Mrs. Withers, leading the way to the couch. "We'll have to talk our secrets at odd moments. Somebody is always bobbing in.... First, I want to tell you two things— that I know will make us friends."

"I hope so—believe so," returned Marian, trying to hold her calm.

"Listen. All my life I've been among the Indians," said Mrs. Withers, in her low voice. "I loved Indians when I was a child. I've been here in this wild country for many years. It takes years of kindness and study to understand the Indian.... These Indians here have come to care for me. They have given me a name. They believe me—trust me. They call on me to settle disputes, to divide property left by their dead, to tell their troubles. I have learned their dreams, their religion, their prayers and legends and poetry, their medicine, the meaning of their dances. And the more I learn of them the more I love and respect them. Indians are not what they appear to most white people. They are children of nature. They have noble hearts and beautiful minds. They have criminals among them, but in much less proportion than have the white race. The song of Hiawatha is true—true for all Indians. They live in a mystic world of enchantment peopled by spirits, voices, music, whisperings of God, eternal and everlasting immortality. They are as simple as little children. They personify everything. With them all is symbolic."

Mrs. Withers paused a moment, her eloquent eyes riveted upon Marian.

"For a good many years this remote part of the Indian country was far out of the way of white men. Thus, the demoralization and degradation of the Indian were retarded, so far as this particular tribe is concerned. This Nopah tribe is the proudest, most intelligent, most numerous, and the wealthiest tribe left in the United States. So-called civilization has not yet reached Kaidab. But it is coming. I feel the next few years will go hard with the Indian—perhaps decide his fate."

"Oh—there seems no hope!" murmured Marian.

"There indeed seems none, if you look at it intelligently and mercilessly. But I look at this question as the Indian looks at everything. He begins his prayer, 'Let all be well with me,' and he ends it, 'Now all is well with me.' He feels—he trusts. There really is a God. If there were not, I would be an infidel. Life on the desert magnified all.... I want you to let me help you to understand the Indian.... For sake of your happiness!"

Marian could not voice her surprise. A tremor ran over her.

"Nophaie showed me your picture—told me about you," went on Mrs. Withers, with an exquisite softness of voice. "Ah! do not be shocked. It was well for him that he confided in me.... I met him the day he returned from the East. I remembered him. I knew him as a boy, a little shepherd who refused to leave his flock in a sandstorm. I know the place where he was born. I know the sage where he was stolen. I knew the horse thief who stole him. I knew the woman who took him East and put him in school.... But Nophaie did not remember me. He went out to the sage slopes of Nothsis Ahn, and when he rode back, he had not his white man's clothes, or speech, or name. He was Nophaie. And he rode here now and then.

The Indians told me about him. He is a chief who wants to help them in a white man's way. But the Indians want him to be a medicine man.... Well, I saw his trouble, and when he came here, I talked. I helped him with his own language. It returned but slowly. I saw his unhappiness. And in the end, he told me about you—showed me your picture—confessed his love."

Marian covered her burning face with trembling hands. She did not mind this good woman knowing her secret, but the truth spoken out, the potent words, the inevitable fact of it being no dream shocked her,

stormed her heart. Nophaie loved her. He had confessed it to this noble friend of the Indians.

"Marian, do not be ashamed of Nophaie's love," went on Mrs. Withers, appealingly. "No one else knows. John suspects, but is not sure. I understand you—feel with you... and I know more. You'd not be here if you did not love Nophaie!"

"Of—course I love—him," said Marian, unsteadily, as she uncovered her face. "You misunderstand. I'm not ashamed.... It's just the shock of hearing---knowing—the suddenness of your disclosure."

"You mustn't mind me—and my knowing all," returned the woman. "This is the desert. You are among primitive peoples. There's nothing complex out here. Your sophistication will fall from you like dead scales."

Gathering courage, and moved by an intense and perfect assurance of sympathy, Marian briefly told Mrs. Withers of her romance with Nophaie, and then of her condition in life and her resolve to have her fling at freedom, to live a while in the West and in helping the Indians perhaps find something of happiness.

Louisa Wetherill, inspiration for Mrs. Withers (Complements of John and Louisa Wetherill Collection)

"Ah! You will grieve, but you will also be wonderfully happy," replied Mrs. Withers. "As for Nophaie—you will save him. His heart was breaking. And when an Indian's heart breaks, he dies.... I kept track of Nophaie. He had a remarkable career in college. He was a splendid student and a great athlete. I've heard that Nophaie's father was a marvelous runner. And he carried the Testing Stone of the braves the farthest for generations.... But what good Nophaie's education and prowess will do out here is a question. He must learn to be an Indian. Eighteen years away made him more white than red. He will never go back to the white man's life.... Marian, I wonder—does that worry you? Be honest with me?"

"No. I would not want him to go back," replied Marian.

"And you said you had no near and dear ties?" queried Mrs. Withers, with her magnetic eyes on Marian's.

"None very near or dear."

"And you were sick of artificial life—of the modern customs—of all that- -"

"Indeed, I was," interrupted Marian.

"And you really have a longing to go back to simple and outdoor ways?"

"Longing!" exclaimed Marian, almost with passion, carried out of self- control by this woman's penetrating power to thrill her. "I—I don't know what it is. But I think under my fair skin—I'm a savage!"

"And you have some money?"

"Oh, I'm not rich, but then I'm not poor, either."

"And you love Nophaie—as you're sure you could never love another man—a white man?"

"I—I love him terribly," whispered Marian. "How can I foretell the future—any possible love—again? But I hate the very thought. Oh, I had it put to me often enough lately—marriage for money or convenience—for a home—for children—for anything but love? No. No! Not for me."

"And will you marry Nophaie?" added Mrs. Withers.

Marian uttered a little gasp. Again, it was not shame that sent the prickling hot blood to her cheeks, but a liberation of emotion she had restrained. This blunt and honest woman called to her very depths.

"Nophaie is an Indian," Mrs. Withers went on. "But he's a man. I never saw a finer man—white or red.... I think you're a fortunate girl. To love and be loved—to live in this desert—to see its wildness and grandeur—to learn of it from an *Indian*—to devote your energies to a noble cause! I hope you see the truth!"

"I don't see very clearly, but I believe you," replied Marian. "You express something vague and deep in me—that wants to come out.... I ought not forget to tell you—Nophaie never asked me to—to marry him."

"Well, it wasn't because he didn't want to, believe me," returned the older woman. "I've seen some lovelorn Indians in my day, but Nophaie beats them all.... What do you think you'll do—send for him or ride out to his home?"

"I—I'd rather meet him out—away—somewhere in the desert," replied Marian, in thoughtful perplexity. "But would that be—be all right? It's so unheard of—this thing I'm doing. I *want* to do it. The strongest feelings in me sanction it. But I'm sensitive—I don't want people to know. Oh, it's the cowardice and deceit of my kind."

"Certainly, it'll be all right. John will take you to meet Nophaie," rejoined Mrs. Withers, warmly. "And no one, except John and me, will be in the secret. We'll tell the men and everyone who happens along that you've come out to work among the Indians."

"Thank you. That will make it easier for me until I find myself.... I was brazen enough when I started out. But my courage seems oozing away."

"I reckon these first days will be hard for you. But don't get blue. All will be well. You're young, healthy, strong. You have a mind. You'll have a wonderful experience out here and be the better, if not the happier for it."

At that juncture Withers came tramping into the room.

"Say, you look like you'd be good medicine," he said heartily, as he stood gazing, somewhat surprised and wholly delighted. "What the desert will do to that complexion!... Well, miss, a Pahute Indian just rode in. He saw Nophaie this morning and talked with him. I thought you'd be glad to hear that."

"Oh—to-day! So near!" exclaimed Marian.

"Shore can't call it near—if you mean where Nophaie is. Nigh on to a hundred miles."

"What did he tell you?" queried Marian, eagerly.

"Not much, I just asked if he'd seen Nophaie. He said he had, at sunup this morning. Nophaie was with the sheep. It's lambing time out there. Nophaie was a great shepherd boy. I've heard before how he goes with the sheep. This Pahute laughed and said, 'Nophaie forgets his white mind and goes back to the days of his youth.' I think all the Indians feel joy over Nophaie's renunciation of the white man's life."

"May I take a look at this Pahute?" asked Marian.

"Come on. I'll introduce you," replied Withers, with a laugh.

"Yes, go out with him," interposed Mrs. Withers. "I must see about dinner."

"I don't want to be introduced or have this Pay—Pahute see I'm interested," said Marian to Withers, as they passed out of the house. "I think it's a matter of sentiment. I just want to—to look at the Indian who saw Nophaie this very day."

"I was only joking, Miss Warner," returned Withers, seriously. "This Pahute is a bad Indian. He's got a record, I'm sorry to say. He's killed white men and Indians both."

"Oh! I've heard or read that fights and bloodshed were things of the past."

"Shore you have," said Withers, with a grim note in his voice. "But you heard or read what's not true. Of course, the frontier isn't wild and bad, as it was forty years ago, when I was a boy. Nor anything so tough as fifteen years ago when the Indians killed my brother. But this border is yet a long way from tame."

He led Marian through the back of the gray stone house into the store. The center of this large room was a stone-floored square, walled off from the spacious and crowded shelves by high counters. Indians were leaning against these counters. Marian saw locks of raven black hair straggling from under dusty crumpled black sombreros. She saw the flash of silver buckles and ornaments. She heard the clink of silver money and low voices, in which the syllable predominating sounded like toa and taa. All these Indians had their backs turned to Marian and appeared to be making purchases of the white man behind the counter. Piles of Indian blankets covered the ends of the counters. Back of them on the shelves were a variety of colored dry goods and canned foods and boxes and jars. From the ceiling hung saddles, bridles, lanterns, lassos—a numberless assortment of articles salable to Indians.

"Here's your Pahute," said Withers, pointing from the doorway out into the open. "Not very pretty, is he?"

Marian peeped out from behind the trader to see a villainous-looking little Indian, black almost, round-faced, big-nosed, with the boldest, hardest look she had ever seen on a human being's face. He wore a high-crowned conical- shaped sombrero, with a wide stiff brim. It was as black as his hair and ornamented with bright beads. His garb consisted of a soiled velvet or corduroy shirt, and trousers of blue jeans. His silver-dotted belt held a heavy gun. A shiny broad silver bracelet circled a sinewy wrist, from which hung a leather quirt. Altogether this Indian was not a pleasant and reassuring sight for the eyes of a city girl, new on the desert. Yet he fascinated Marian.

"Well, what do you think of him?" asked Withers, smiling.

"I'm not especially taken with him," replied Marian, with a grimace. "I prefer to see him at a distance. But he looks—like—"

"Like the real thing. You bet he is. But to give the devil his due, this Pahute hasn't done a mean or vicious thing since Nophaie came back. The Indians tell me Nophaie has talked good medicine to him."

"What is this medicine?" asked Marian.

"The Indians make medicine out of flowers, roots, bark, herbs, and use it for ills the same as white people do. But medicine also means prayer, straight talk, mystic power of the medicine men of the tribe and their use of sand paintings."

"What are they?"

"When the medicine man comes to visit a sick Indian, he makes paintings on a flat rock with different colored sands. He paints his message to the Great Spirit. These paintings are beautiful and artistic. But few white people have ever seen them. And the wonderful thing is that the use of them nearly always cures the sick Indian."

"Then Nophaie has begun to help his people?"

"He shore has."

"I am very glad," said Marian, softly. "I remember he always believed he could not do any good."

"We're glad, too. You see, Miss Warner, though we live off the Indians, we're honestly working for them."

"The trader at Mesa said much the same, and that traders were the only friends the Indians had. Is it true?"

"We believe so. But I've known some missionaries who were honest-to-God men—who benefited the Indians."

"Don't they *all* work for the welfare of the Indians?"

The trader gave her a keen, searching look, as if her query was one often put to him, and which required tact in answering.

"Unfortunately, they do not," he replied, bluntly. "Reckon in every walk of life there are men who betray their calling. Naturally we don't expect that of missionaries. But in Morgan and Friel we find these exceptions. They are bad medicine. The harm they do, in many cases, is counteracted by the efforts of missionaries who work sincerely for the good of the Indian. As a matter of fact, some of the missionaries don't last long out here, unless they give in to Morgan's domination."

"Why, that seems strange!" said Marian, wonderingly. "Has this Morgan power to interfere with really good missionaries?"

"Has he?" replied Withers, with grim humor. "I reckon. He tries to get rid of missionaries he can't rule, or, for that matter, *anybody*."

"How in the world can he do that?" demanded Marian, with spirit.

"Nobody knows, really. But we who have been long on the reservation have our ideas. Morgan's power might be politics or it might be church—or both. Shore he stands ace high with the Mission Board in the East. There's no doubt about the Mission Board being made up of earnest churchmen who seek to help and Christianize the Indians. I met one of them—the president. He would believe any criticism of Morgan to be an attack from a jealous missionary or a religious clique of another church. The *facts* never get to this mission board. That must be the cause of Morgan's power. Someday the scales will fall from their eyes and they'll dismiss him."

"How very different—this missionary work— from what we read and hear!" murmured Marian, dreamily thinking of Nophaie's letter.

"I reckon it is," said Withers. "Miss Warner, do you want me to send a message or letter to Nophaie by this Pahute?" inquired Withers. "He'll ride out to-morrow."

"No. I'd rather go myself," replied Marian. "Mrs. Withers said you'd take me. Will you be so kind?"

"I shore'll take you," he rejoined. "I've got some sheep out that way, and other interests. It's a long ride for a tenderfoot. How are you on a horse?"

"I've ridden some, and this last month I went to a riding school three times a week. I'm pretty well hardened. But of course, I can't really *ride*. I can learn, though."

"It's well you broke in a little before coming West. Because these Nopah trails are rough riding, and you'll have all you can stand. When would you like to start?"

"Just as soon as you can."

"Day after tomorrow, then. But don't set your heart on surprising Nophaie. It can't be done."

"Why? If we tell no one?"

"Things travel ahead of you in this desert. It seems the very birds carry news. Some Indian will see us on the way, ride past us, or tell another Indian. And it'll get to Nophaie before we do."

"What will get to Nophaie?"

"Word that trader Withers is riding west with Benow di cleash. Shore, won't that make Nophaie think?"

"He'll know," said Marian, tensely.

"Shore. He'll ride to meet you. I'll take you over the Pahute trail. You'll be the first white person except myself ever to ride it. You need nerve, girl."

"Must I? Oh, my vaunted confidence! My foolish little vanity! Mr. Withers, I'm scared of it all—the bigness, the strangeness of this desert—of what I must do."

"Shore you are. That's only natural. Begin right now. Use your eyes and sense. Don't worry. Take things as they come. Make up your mind to stand them. All will be well."

Then from the doorway Mrs. Withers called her to supper.

Zane Grey

*Dolly Grey (L. Tom Perry Collection, BYU, MSS
6081, Box 37, Folder 4)*

CHAPTER 11
DOLLY GREY

From Dolly Grey's Personal Notes (1917)

This chapter on Dolly Grey is different from Zane Grey's heroine stories in that it was written by Dolly herself! It is included here to provide additional perspective on a woman who truly was a heroine in Grey's life.

In 1917, Dolly, Zane and two of Grey's "secretaries" took a trip by train across America to visit Glacier National Park then continue to the Pacific Coast. The journey passed through Washington's wheat country and inspired the novel The Desert of Wheat.

This chapter shares Dolly Grey's notes from the trip transcribed from the original in the archives of the L. Tom Perry Collections at Brigham Young University. (MSS 8710, Box 6, Item 3). Included are images recently gifted to Zane Grey's West Society from the same journey.

Dolly's account is important for several reasons. First, it helps confirm places Grey visited that were previously unclear. Secondly, the notes shed some light on the relationship between Dolly and at least two of Grey's "secretaries." Finally, you will enjoy Dolly's writing style which meshed well with Grey's stories as she edited them.

PART ONE:
GLACIER BY RAIL

July 7, 1917

IT SEEMS PASSING STRANGE to be flying away from my "nearest and dearest" as poor old Herman Gebbard used to term them. Again, I have that feeling a thread between my heart and theirs - a thread as thin as a spider's, which stretches and stretches as the distance increases and always pulls a little more and hurts a little more. Why is life as it is? Why must we always choose? Why can't we go along smoothly and comfortably without suffering? Why must I leave my children or be left by my husband? It is far harder to be left than to leave. Being left is agonizing, I'm learning there is always something new something beckoning ahead - there is more over the joy of going home.

I have taken out my babies' pictures and looked at them and at Loren's kiss curl. How many times have I kissed it, that dear little curl at the back of his neck? I had to take it with me. I can hear him say it - "Kiss curl."

They were all just through with their evening scrub when I kissed them goodbye. Betty said "Will you bring me something, Mother?" Then she patted my face several times and gave me a tremendous hug, but all the time the little imps were dancing in her eyes. Romer was more serious.

Ida and Elma went to the train with us. I think, I know, Elma felt pretty badly, but she's spunky and proud. When we passed the house, they were all on the back steps waving to us. I can't describe the feeling I had.

We are just out of Binghamton and all tucked away in our berths.

As long as it was light, I looked out of the window. The upper reaches of the Delaware are perfectly beautiful. For a while the country is softer, flatter more pastoral than at Lackawaxen. Then it grows more mountainous again, but still in a softer way. I have never seen such beautiful luxuriantly wooded hills. And the river winds and curves among them revealing new beauties at each turn. At Hancock the river divided into the East and West Branches. The East left us, and we continued to follow the west for a while.

All the way up the river, the lack of towns, even houses struck me. The country seems almost virgin, for those wonderful hills have never been cut over.

I'll try to sleep now. I've had a difficult day. Between a raging headache and a system full of suppressed emotion, I was near the breaking point. I wonder why Romer didn't send me the candy? Did he forget?

July 8, 1917

The night wasn't very good for me, but towards morning I got some better sleep. Just when I had entirely lost myself something hit me in the stomach - Doc's foot - murdered sleep. So, I read for an hour and then got up at 8.

Morning in Ohio. It had rained during the night and it's a gray day, but cool and pleasant for traveling. My last trip through Ohio was in the dead of winter. Then, as now, the towns, villages, houses struck me as dingy and ugly, but the country is soft and rolling and fertile looking - good farm country. There is some wheat, just beginning to turn. The corn seems small for this time of year. I haven't seen any potatoes yet, farther East in Pennsylvania, there were quantities of them.

Some idea of the wealth of all this beautiful undeveloped country gets to me as we travel over the miles. I don't suppose there is an inch of it that, would not, in some way yield something for the good of man. And yet there are miles on miles where not a human habitation is to be seen. Ohio is populous of course, but not the part of Pa. I saw.

This morning in the dressing room, a tall motherly woman, with a little girl, spoke to me. She said this was the fifth time she had been over the Erie since January, for sickness and death, etc. She had buried her oldest boy -12 - three months ago. Said she didn't have any luck with her children. That she'd lost all but this little girl. She didn't whine about it, thought, and said she'd reconciled herself to it.

There is another interesting looking family. They don't look American, but speak like cultured ones. The mother is a little shriveled old woman to whom the young son seems very devoted. He often sits with his arm around her and she looks blissfully happy. Then there are two girls; the younger about sixteen, pretty, resembling Anna Wood; the elder, homely, but interesting and intellectual looking. They both are college girls, I think, from the snatches of conversation. There is an older man, who, I think is the father.

St. Paul
July 9, 1917

We got in here at seven this morning, after changing yesterday evening at Chicago.

After twelve o'clock 1 was wakeful, and as soon as I realized what beautiful country we were passing through, I took cat-naps and looked out the rest of the time, for it was moonlight. This Minnesota is a beautiful state. I saw every kind of inland water, which of course, all go to swell the great "Father of Waters." And the beautiful fertile fields of wheat and oats and clover, and everything! Then there are woods and hills and no lack of variety. Presently we were traveling along the Mississippi which meandered and spread and separated between low-lying bluffs about a mile apart. And oh, the wonderful look of it. With a rush came back my desire to take a houseboat trip down the Mississippi. Someday, I'll do it with all the children, and we'll fish and loaf and explore. I wish I had words to describe the beauty of it all. But I couldn't. I just lay in my berth and looked. And presently the great red sun came up – it was very early - about 4:30 and then I got up also. I knocked at Doc's berth above me, thinking he wouldn't like to miss it all, but he didn't answer and when I got up, he was still tight asleep.

There was one particularly beautiful place called Red Wing, a good name for it.

In St. Paul we sat at a lunch counter in a tacky little place and had a bit of breakfast. Then we started out to explore the town; but Doc isn't strong on exploring towns, and after going to the Great Northern Ticket Office and buying an electric iron and a few notebooks, he led us back to the station.

St. Paul, or its environs is evidently not suffering from race suicide, for almost every woman had a child or two. The people here all look like farmers. I didn't see a well-dressed woman or man all the time I was here.

I persuaded Doc we needed a second walk for health's sake and we strolled out on one of the bridges over the Mississippi. It gave me a peculiar thrill to be standing over the big river and to think of where it went. Lots of things thrill me, and thank goodness, I am still intensely interested in everything and everybody. I hope I will never cease to be.

The train is leaving now. The Oriental Limited -much advertised - and well crowded. Doc is fussing because the girls' section is not opposite ours, but perhaps that can be changed. It's difficult to write on the train, or I'd write more. And if I wait too long, I lose interest.

There were wonderful exhibits of wheat, fruits and foodstuffs in the Great Northern office, and all from the country through which we pass.

1905 photo of a train passing through Red Wing, MN. (Photo courtesy of Red Wing Shoes)

Tuesday
July 10, 1917

Yesterday was a warm crowded, rather uncomfortable, but overall interesting day. Minnesota is a beautiful state but after a while, the landscape repeats itself indefinitely though attractively. There are many lakes, great wheat and farm fields, attractive farm buildings, and that the people have an eye for beauty is shown by the clumps of trees and woods that make a pattern of the landscape.

Towards evening we got into North Dakota, which simply repeated Minnesota, until it got too dark to see. I rather wish we had stopped at Fargo as first planned. It looked like a clean, breezy, attractive, typically western, town with which I would have liked to become acquainted.

This morning we awakened in Montana and lost another hour - that is, turned back our watches; It was my first good night's sleep.

We are getting suggestions of the bare western mountains on the horizon, I don't like them. They give me an aching, awesome, empty feeling that is uncomfortable. To me they are like great suffering naked Titans, Give me my home hills with their richness of soft green covering. These great mountains here denote some awful cataclysmic upheaval of bygone ages. Beside them man is less than a creeping ant. Maybe that's why I don't like them. Maybe my ego objects to the puny, ant-like frame of mind. But they truly do hurt me. When I feel small or insignificant, I want the feeling to be cosmic. Then it elevates me.

For some time, we paralleled the Missouri River but it does not seem to enrich the soil here. There is some wheat, among which grow many black-eyed Susans; the occasional greener patches are of alfalfa; mostly there are great stretches of yellowish green grass. It is probably a grazing country, though so far, I've seen few cattle. Back a way was an Indian Reservation and we saw their tents and horses and squaws. One Indian sat his horse stolid and motionless, back turned, and never even bothered to look at the train.

Here and there, at long intervals, is a settlement of wooden shacks, tents, anything put or thrown together for shelter. Some have mud roofs out of which grass grows. There is quite a bit of sage too. The most pathetic thing I saw was a small American flag bravely waving in the breeze over a tiny house made of black tar paper and held together by a few lathes.

Just now we're passing at intervals great flocks of sheep. They are beautiful, and it's no wonder that artists like to paint them. At a great distance here, on this almost desert coloring, they book almost like a field of puffy dandelions gone to seed.

It is rather an over-cast day and the sky has beautiful tints and colorings. And when, occasionally, one gets a glimpse of distant dark blue mountains, it emphasizes everything exquisitely. That's what this monotony of country needs - emphasis. And one gets just enough of it to whet the appetite. Nature is a wonderful landscape artist.

Dolly Grey was describing shacks like this one provided courtesy of the State Historic Society of North Dakota CO694

Doc got fussy and angry yesterday because we stayed in the observation car for several hours. It was pleasant and cool and comfortable there, and at 4:30 they served afternoon tea. Then we got back. Doc had an exceedingly injured expression on his face. He asked me if the girls had talked to anyone. He's always worrying about them and that sort of thing. I finally asked him whether he didn't trust Mildred, but he'd trust Dot anywhere.

Before I knew it, I burst out "As a matter of fact, Mildred is to be trusted every bit as much as Dot, and Dot always has a much more peculiar expression on her face than Mil has, when a man appears."

The minute I said it, I was sorry, but it's as true as gospel. Both of them are ready for fun of that kind. Mildred is more open about it and Dot is slyer.

They've always done it, and the only reason they refrain from it now is because of Doc. Their expression when an eligible man appears is exceedingly interesting and amusing to me. And I

don't blame them in a way. If they do nothing wrong or harmful, why should I quarrel with their way of having a good time. Of course, they wouldn't pick up anyone when I'm around, but I claim it's the look and expression in their eyes and faces that invites men just as plainly as words would. And Dot has more come-hither eyes than Mildred.

Poor Doc, he takes things too hard, he'll have a great awakening someday. But I'm going to try as hard as I can to make everything pleasant for him this trip and I spoke to Mildred about it. She was perfectly frank and said she and Dot liked to get acquainted with new fellows, but of course they wouldn't do anything like that because of Doc. And Doc always blames the men for it. You'd think they were ravening wolves. I say it's up to the girls.

There was a beautiful young girl on the train yesterday. She had something of Allie Benke, Jo Munson and Emmeline, but was prettier than any of them. When Doc saw her, he remarked "It's a good thing Uncle Romer isn't on the train alone." As a matter of fact, I would have trusted Romer sooner than Doc. Half an hour with that girl would have finished Doc, regardless of Dottie.

Dottie and Doc are both off color this morning. Poor Dot has had four upheavals and Doc's been having awful dreams in which Elma tells him he's an old has-been. That is abysmal tragedy for Doc, even in dreams.

Zane and Dolly Grey were accompanied West in 1917 by two of the author's "secretaries/companions", Dorothy Ackerman (left) and Mildred Ferguson

The dinner was too crowded to allow our being together and Mildred and I were separated from the others. Mildred and I ordered a light, conservative meal, but the other two were steered into full dinner by which the road advertises itself. They did it up from soup to nuts, and when Mildred and I left the diner, they were entirely surrounded by strawberry shortcake, whipped cream, and ice cream, no wonder!

Horses among the sage!
How that thrills me.

We are stopping now at a garage and a sign, which advertises irrigated land and homesteads for sale cheap. When I see these vast stretches of unoccupied land, and think of the hordes in Europe fighting, wallowing in blood, killing each other because they haven't enough room to expand, I wonder where the equity, the balance of Nature comes in; For Nature inevitably balances, though God seems not to. Probably that is the relentlessness of Nature seeking her balance over there. Men have been getting too far away from her, and paradoxically, over-crowding her. And so, the upheaval.

Yesterday when I was playing cards with the girls, I became conscious of a woman's voice back of me, rising and falling with all. The inflections and sibilant hisses, etc. of the cheap orator. Presently the voice became so loud, and the contents of the talk so interesting, that we couldn't give our attentions to the cards. Such expressions as "What are we fighting for? So, Mr. Pierrrrrpont Morrrrgan doesn't lose the millions he invested in England." - Oh, the scorn in those tones!

I looked around. It was a big, raw-boned, mannish looking woman I'd noticed earlier and she was orating to three scared, shrivelled-looking shrimps of women who acted as a Greek chorus. Well, I never heard such traitorous talk in all my life. It appears that the lady has an only son, who she said she had raised "as carefully as a girl, and who had tender instincts." It appears that the son has enlisted (from her talk one would think he'd been dragged in by the hair, but my private opinion is that he went of his own accord) at any rate, his lady mother chooses to make it the reason for reviling all of America - our government and particularly President Wilson whom she called a "Squaw-man" , and Mrs. Wilson! What right had that woman to tell her she should eat cornbread, and go without one meal a day. Humph!

Then the voice would sink to a heart-rending stage whisper with a tearing sigh about the poorrr motherrr and the butchered boys and what was it for! So, England-- oh, I forget it all, but she had all the stock arguments. Wilson never was fair. That's why Bryan quit, when Wilson refused to call England for the same reason he called Germany. What did we fight the war of 1812 for? For the same thing that England was doing now. Well, it's useless to repeat it all. By this time I was getting awfully riled up myself, and I was crazy to jump in, but Doc said for me not to, and I suppose it was wiser, but if any man had gotten off that talk, he would have been lassoed and bumped along from the end of this train; providing any other man had heard him.

And I suppose because a woman like that has a son in the army or wherever he is, they couldn't touch her. And she'd probably whine and take advantage of that.

There are too very fat ladies with one very lean husband from Cincinnati, in the next section from us. They smile very pleasantly at me and I feel that they're dying to exchange the stories of our lives. What makes me like them is that they have a sense of humor. When the lady orator was holding forth,

I looked at them, and they and I both burst out laughing. And since then there has been a little feeling of understanding.

Back in the compartment car is a little greasy man with long hair brushed straight back. A Vandyke beard, and flowing black tie, after the manner of would-be (and some real) geniuses. He has a nice-looking wife, and what irritates me is that just that silly make-up interests me and other people by creating wonder as to who he is and if he really is a somebody. A man like that must be entirely devoid of a sense of humor, or he must be crafty enough to know that he attracts attention, or he must really be a somebody. Anyway, people look at him and wonder.

In the drawing room are a man and his wife who. Doc says, look like a Chicago politician and his wife. The man is big, authoritative looking, yet rather a pleasant face, the woman bedazzled, rather over-dressed. Their son, a young fellow of about sixteen or so, sat in the section opposite us. He looks a little bit like mama's boy, but has good stuff, I think, and gave me a nice smile when he picked up my pillow. And there, too, I saw the sense of humor. I'd like to talk to him, but Doc would think I was picking up something for the girls. I'd talk to everyone if it wasn't for that. It's the human contacts that are broadening and education. This eternal dragging in of the idea of sex and men are really much more interesting to talk to than women.

Well, I'll knit some more. My sock is growing. I can understand Madame Defarge.

Evening

We're nearing Glacier Park now and on the distant horizon the mountains are appearing, great bold blue peaks that must be thirty or more miles away, with cattle ranges in between. They are huge and wonderful and grand. They make me ache. Some of them seem to have snow.

From; the sublime to the ridiculous. -I can't leave this chronicle of our journey without mentioning Doc's pants. He was very spruce and neat-looking when we left home in his linen trousers, dark coat, and white shoes and socks. Next day they began to wrinkle and when we got into Chicago, they were loose and baggy and like a Chinaman's. Doc began to worry about them, then, and he's been worrying ever since. Finally, a couple of hours ago, he made up his mind to change them, and he's been uncomfortable ever since, too dressed up.

At dinner tonight we talked to rather an interesting Westerner - tanned, clear-eyed, decisive. These Western men are fine types.

There is an absolutely typical cowman aboard – and also a typical miner.

We have less than an hour now. This, to me, has been a very interesting day, and I've kept busy every minute.

We passed quite a freight wreck at Chester. Engine and train completely smashed and turned over at sides of track. Don't know cause, but it held us up awhile.

Just very suddenly, we felt the cool mountain air and smelled it and we're climbing all the time now, heading right into that great wall. Oh, it's wonderful.

We had a grouchy condescending porter this trip, but he shined up to Doc and told him there were a lot of cheap tourists on the train, but he knew the real thing when saw it! Quite the compliment to us! Notice he's also shined up to the wealthy party. Such is life!!

How grateful the land is for a little water and how quickly it shows its appreciation. We are passing just now through a sort of oasis through which a branch of the Missouri meanders. There is fresh green grass, the trees are plentiful and shady and in the prettiest spot, a little new village of small modern houses is springing up. There are even a church and a schoolhouse, white-painted and trim. I notice many schoolhouses through this state and they are all large and fine and seemingly all out of proportion to the few and lovely-looking habitations.

I have wondered whether suffrage could have anything to do with this. These states are both enfranchised. At any rate, the same spirit that has given women the vote must have built these attractive schools. Last night a woman of this country with two young children got on the train. She would typify my idea of what women of this country should be. Strong, healthy, and handsome,

1917 Montana Schoolhouse
(Courtesy Montana State Historical Society)

tanned as beautifully brown as her two young ones, with fine hard-working hands. She had the look of the pioneer woman, the woman who is the salt of the earth, the kind of woman that God must have meant all women to be. She was rather serious and shy and ill at ease among all the people here, and she told me it was rather hard to travel alone with the two children. They too were shy. While I tried to make friends with them. The little fellow looked like Betty. They all piled into an upper berth and we heard the children once or twice but this morning, they were gone.

In a country like this, conditions are reversed. The towns and human habitations become the interesting things for they break the monotony of the vast, never-ending stretches of land. Take this little town of Glasgow, for instance. It seems quite important. On the main street, which runs along the railroad, are several attractive brick business buildings and of course innumerable saloons. Right on the station platform is a little round glass building with a fine wheat exhibit, and the bags of flour marked Glasgow, Mont. indicate the cause for the town's existence. And the people one sees here. The burned, hardy, strong-looking people with the open look that fits the open country

Glacier Park

Seeing much beautiful scenery is like trying to choose a hat or a dress. The first one that you like seems just right and not to be surpassed; then as you see more and more, you don't know which you like best. So it was with Glacier National Park. When we got off the train, we saw a huge, Swiss-style building in the distance. We walked under a great rustic arch, up a poppy-bordered path to the hotel, which is entirely constructed of great trees and logs and which carries out the construction in every detail. Instead of columns, enormous tree trunks supported the roof, both inside and out. The interior was beautiful, and Indian rugs, bear-skins, log fires, carried out the general scheme. In the long sun-parlor and dining room, the great windows made frames for the scenery, one picture more beautiful than the next.

Everything was harmonious and pleasing and made me feel good. That first evening we hung around and looked at some moving pictures of the park and Indians – the Blackfeet Indians on whose reservation the Glacier Park Hotel stands. It appears that Glacier National Park was ceded to the government by one of the Blackfeet chiefs. Later we met his son.

Next morning, we wrote quantities of letters and postcards, then took a walk up a beautiful mountain stream, but the flies, bugs and mosquitoes were a pest. We saw and picked at least twenty different varieties of the most beautiful wild flowers, many of which I recognized from my I,ackawaxen botanizing.

*Zane Grey's 1917 companions 1) in front of the Glacier Park
Lodge; 2) on the porch of Glacier Lake Lodge; and 3) at the
entrance to Glacier Lake Lodge.*

PART 2:
GLACIER TO THE PACIFIC

DOC MET MR. MILLS, one the head men of the Great Northern, and he proposed taking us in his auto to the principal points of interest in the park. So about seven next morning we started out. With us was a Mr. Ulke, a scientist, whom Mr. Mills asked our permission to take, and we were mighty glad to have him, for as a source of information he was unsurpassed.

The car was a big white - seven-passenger, and we had a splendid chauffeur. We flew exceedingly fast, up and down, and around terribly dangerous curves where any least turn would have shot us thousands of feet into eternity. I wasn't at all nervous or scared, strange to say. Twice we crossed a stream on two planks! Some driving. First, we went 24 miles to Two Medicine Lakes.

On the way we dropped Mr. Ulke and Doc at a stream in the woods to do a little trout-fishing. At Two Medicine Lakes we got off, took a few pictures, All these lakes are surrounded by the lowering peaks which are reflected in them when the wind doesn't blow. Groups of chalets perch the shores and on high places over-looking the lakes. We didn't linger long at this first place, but got off where we had left Doc and walked through the woods along the brook. The girls were wearing their high-heeled slippers and Dot's heel came off. Mr. Mills hammered it on with a stone, Meanwhile the mosquitoes almost ate us. Again, we were compensated when we saw Trick Falls - a double water-fall half of which comes over the top of the mountain, and the rest from a cavern on the hillside. Mr. Ulke had caught one small cut-throat trout, which he carried with him. Doc had had several good bites.

Zane Grey fishing in Glacier National Park,
likely with the scientist, Ulke

From there we dashed along at great speed in order to get the boat at St. Mary's at 11:15. I cannot attempt to describe the wonderful panorama. There was every combination which lakes, rivers, streams, pine-clad forests, mountain meadows, and the wonderful titanic, rock-ribbed peaks could devise, and we shot up and down and all around. Many of the streams we forded.

Finding what a wonderful course in Popular Science Mr. Ulke could be, I took advantage of his presence to find out ever thing I possibly could, especially about the geology of the region. Geology had, of course, always been intensely interesting to me, and I haven't forgotten as much as I thought. I heard Mr. Ulke tell Doc that I was quite a geologist, and Doc told me later he said I was a "charmingly cultured woman", which, of course, pleased me much, though I know it's conceited to write it down. Mr. Ulke is completely informed in every branch of science. He is in the government Patent Office - expert in chemistry section, and now on his trip he's botanizing and classifying the flora and fauna. But he's also been geologist and mineralogist, mining expert, forester, everything - and he can impart his information so that it's intensely interesting. And with it he has a sense of humor, and he's very funny, and sort of naive so one has to laugh at him. His greatest fault appears to be talking too much, but I think he's so full of information that it has to bubble out. And he's always gathering more.

Every time we stopped, he'd shoot out of the car and pick some new flower or leaf or something. At St. Mary's he jumped off the launch lust as it was ready to leave, scrambled up the steep hillside and brought me back a rare lily - Clintonia Uniflora. And he's the same way about people - talks to everybody - pumps them dry. Never 'til the last second would he leave a place. Doc was very much taken with him and they want to take a trip and write a book together. A man like that would be very valuable to Doc, besides affording a lot of amusement.

Even if the Professor had only five minutes at a brook, he'd cut a switch, put a thread hook on it and start fishing. Doc lent him a fly-rod and he didn't know how to handle it. Also, he lost the reel, and confessed it for all the world like a naughty child. And when Doc was nice about it, his face cleared and he laughed. He confided to me afterward that he feared he'd "catch it" for losing the reel.

Mr. Ulke is a bachelor and his home in Washington, D.C, is kept by some old maid sisters. He told us about a couple of matrimonial escapes he'd had, but he's still on the lookout for a congenial mate, who will share his interests, I should say the lady would have to be some mountain climber. Mr., Ulke is the typical scientist in appearance. On the launch it struck me, when the three men were standing together, how perfect an example each was of his type – Mr. Mills the big business man. Mr. Ulke, the scientist, and Doc the novelist. It was striking.

At about 11:15 AM, we left for St. Mary's Lake and there took the launch up the lake to the "Going to the Sun" chalets. This St. Mary's Lake, or rather two lakes, are very long, and the mountains rise right out of them. The boat-ride to the upper end of one lake took about an hour.

(R-L) Mr, Ulke with Zane's fishing rod, Mr. Mills, Dorothy Ackerman, Dolly Grey, Mildred Ferguson and unidentified young man.

A steep climb from, the landing brought us to the chalets, where we had a beautiful view of "Going to the Sun Mountain". There was a high rocky island in the lake and later Mr. Mills had the launch take the extra little trip above that. Here the scenery was particularly fine.

We had luncheon here, and the waitress brought in an enormous, elaborately decorated platter, in the middle of which reposed Mr. Ulke's wee cut-throated (cutthroat) trout. This he insisted I eat all, myself. It was delicious. Later we returned to St. Mary's and found that our chauffeur had caught a large Mackinaw trout in our absence. This he also presented to us and the five of us dined on it that night.

From St. Mary's, we went on to Many Glaciers. This to me was the most interesting and thrilling part of the ride. Many a time I held my breath as we swooped around those mountain curves, with eternity hanging just on the driver's care. Along here we saw many Indians and at one place stopped and shook hands with Owen Heavybreast - felicitously named. He was a fat, jolly looking Indian who grinned at us and spoke a fair English, but with the guttural Indian expression.

Chief Owen Heavy Breast (George Grantham Bain Collection, Library of Congress)

The Many Glaciers Hotel on the banks of McDermott Lake is another beautiful place. Mr. Mills had them give us two beautiful rooms with big stone fireplaces and a balcony right over the lake. Doc was so taken with the beds that I made a sketch of them. Mr. Kuhn can make them.

I think I liked this Many Glaciers Place best of all, in spite of the fiendish mosquitoes. The exquisite calm lake surrounded by great rocky peaks which mirrored themselves in it, the rainbow colors of the sunset, all wove a sort of spell around me which none of the other places did. I have changed my mind about these mountains. They no longer intimidate me. I love their ruggedness, their impatient shaking off of the encroaching forests, 'till they rise up bare, craggy, magnificent. The only thing they tolerate is the clouds. Sometimes these envelop them in the softiest, fleeciest way, lying along the summit like folds of chiffon. I did so want to see a thunder storm among the peaks and I had my wish, though they say it occurs very rarely. It was a grand sight - anyone who would not thrill to it must be absolutely callous.

Next morning, Doc suggested climbing one of the mountains, but I thought it would be lots more fun to fish in the lake. Everyone told us that the trout couldn't be caught, but I thought it would be worth trying. So, we trolled across the lake to where the Swift Current (fitly named) entered it and there we cast. Presently Doc had a bite and caught a dandy Rainbow Trout – about 2 lbs. Then I caught one almost as large - great fun, for they were very gamy and leaped and fought. Then I had two more bites - the second a whopper. Oh, if I could only have gotten him! My cup of joy would have over-flowed. About this time the storm was arising and the wind beginning to blow hard, and it wasn't easy to get back across it, to the hotel. Oh, that storm! I watched it until we had to get ready to leave.

Mildred, Dorothy and Dolly admiring view mountain across Lake
McDermott from Many Glacier Hotel
(Courtesy of Zane Grey's West Society)

We went back in the bus, and found it most comfortable riding, except that the storm had made It much colder and we had to bundle up. And all the way home the rain chased us over this mountain and that - never quite getting us except for a few drops. It was an unusual experience. We arrived at Glacier Park on schedule time and pretty well tired out, so we turned in early. The Prof, wanted us to dance, but Doc wouldn't let us.

Next morning, we had to leave. I was sorry and hope I'll get there again some time. They treated us splendidly and wouldn't accept a cent of payment.

While we were waiting for the train, Mr. Mills brought up two wonderfully dressed chiefs and Owen Heavybreast, who all shook hands with us and grinned in friendly fashion. No, after all, only Owen grinned. The others just barely smiled in a most stately way, which was nevertheless friendly. Those wonderful, copper, craggy faces. They fitted their mountains.

Our train was late - Mr. Ulke came to see us off, tickled to death because he had found someone to put in his tooth, the barber, I think. Did I say that while we were having dinner at "Many Glaciers" he bit an olive and one of his false teeth came out? He was very much concerned, but not at all embarrassed, and though we all sort of tried to pass it over without noticing, he came back to the topic. For all the world, I was reminded of Crane. They were similar, both splendid travelers, acquisitive, kindly, and broadly interesting.

The girls have been gathering up everything possible - especially great bunches of writing paper. In all these places the paper is attractive. Posters, soap, meal-tickets, nothing is despised. Doc got them each a notebook, and they're trying to keep a diary. Mildred's will evidently be exhaustive for she borrowed my list of flowers and has been asking me innumerable questions about geology, the flora and fauna, in fact everything we discussed on the trip. She told me she even put down our overwhelming and frequent desire to pinkie. That was a funny thing.

Zane and Dolly Grey fishing at the mouth of Swift Creek on Lake McDermott

I don't know whether the altitude or the water caused it, but if we waited more than an hour, we almost died.

Saturday, July 14, 1917

We left Glacier Park this morning. I had no chance to write any notes there and I doubt if I'll get very far on this shaky train.

We were all so very tired that we went right to sleep as soon as we got aboard, but I couldn't stay so for fear of missing the beautiful scenery. We began to go downhill and the topography changed, began to soften. The trees became more plentiful, the mountains were forest-covered, and there were waters of every kind. For some time, we followed the beautiful Flathead River, a stream of green milky glacial water, full of rapids - swirls, yet navigable in a flat boat. In imagination I shot every fall, and caught all the fish I wanted. I hope we'll get to fish it someday.

Then there were lakes - sapphire and emerald, large and small, and brooks that must have been full of trout, with the clearest of water, showing pebbly bottoms of variegated colorings. And always the pine-clad hills - nothing but pine and spruce and fir; and occasionally small trees of the poplar variety.

And now we are following the Kootenay, swift and muddy. This part of Montana seems to be a great lumbering region. The lakes are full of logs and almost every settlement has a lumber mill. Even so, there is so much pine that one scarcely sees any depletion. In spite of the beautiful scenery, this is an awfully dirty uncomfortable ride.

The girls and I have played bridge for a while, but the time doesn't seem to pass. We didn't eat any lunch today for we had a big breakfast at the hotel.

Just now the porter told we lost another hour before dinner. What a wail! I feel as if I couldn't be seen for the dirt on me. Guess I'll knit. Too shaky to write.

Editor's Note: The Greys were in Spokane, Washington from July 14-18 leaving on the 19th. While in Spokane, they stayed at the famous Davenport Hotel where Zane spoke to the local Chamber of Commerce and learned about the IWW strikes in Washington's wheat fields. These strikes were the inspiration for Grey's novel, The Desert of Wheat. Though Dolly does not mention actually visiting the wheat fields, it's clear that Zane and the ladies did spend time there as documented by the following photographs.

Many of the sawmills the Grey party passed were involved in IWW (Wobbly) strikes in 1917. Zane Grey likely knew since he mentioned the timber strikes in The Desert of Wheat *published later that year.*
(Source: "Industrial Worker," August 25, 1917)

Combine with the rotating reel "header" attached so it is both a thresher and header "combined" and taken around and around by Horses or mules through the field to cut and thresh the grain.

Header box wagon on the left and the header on the right that is cutting grain and dumping it into the wagon. There was a wood-ribbed canvas feeder would around two wooden rollers that carried the grain stalks up from the cutter bar platform and into the header box for transport to the stationary thresher. (Source: Zane Grey's West Society; explanations provided by Richard Scheuerman.)

(left) Zane Grey is standing where the sack-sewer set down the 140-pound sacks of wheat until several high which were then pushed onto the ground for pickup by wagon. The mechanism seen above them is the clean grain auger apparatus. (right top) Grey party leaving Hotel Wheeler in the heart of wheat country (right bottom) Ladies in Zane Grey party looking at wheat falling from the "clean grain return" which brings the winnowed kernels up from the threshing mechanism in the center of the combine to drop them into a metal pipe that empties into the grain sacks. (Images compliments of Zane Grey's West Society; explanation provided by Richard Scheuerman.)

July 19, 1917

We left Spokane on Thursday evening (July 19th) and when we got on the train, I missed my pocketbook - with quite a bit of money in it. We had only ten minutes to spare. There were only two places I could have left it - the moving picture place or the car in which we drove to the station. Doc, with his usual pessimism, said I'd never see it again. But I begged him at least to telephone the Davenport and ask them to look in the car and the movie place and if they found it to send it on to Frisco. He rushed back to the station and did so. We were all sitting in our made-up berths talking about it, waiting for the train to start when a young man cane rushing through asking for Zane Grey - and handed my pocketbook to me. The hotel people had searched the car and rushed it right over. Talk about luck! And it was the culminating touch of my good impression of, and liking for, Spokane.

Next morning when we awoke, we found ourselves in the valley of the Columbia, not far from Portland. Unfortunately, I missed seeing Mt. Hood as I was dressing, but the Cascades were great, with the river winding among them. Gradually the hills became lower as we followed the river down. Some of the rock formations were very interesting - sugar loaf effects, sometimes sticking right up out of the river.

From Portland, the Grey party traveled south to San Francisco where they learned of Grey's mother's death. The ladies headed home to take care of details surrounding the lady's passing. They travelled on what Dolly described as "the Roaring UP Trail" assuredly inspired by her husband's story of the same name. Zane Grey continued his trip in the West including an adventure in the Flathead Mountains of Northern

Colorado that inspired his novel, The Mysterious Rider.

Zane Grey looking at Multnomah Falls

Top: Dolly, Dorothy and Mildred looking at Multnomah Falls;
Bottom: Zane and Dolly walking on the road to Multnomah Falls

Multnomah Falls

Latourell Falls

*Louisa Wetherill talking with Native American friends
(ZGWS Collection)*

CHAPTER 12

LOUISA WETHERILL

From "Slim Woman of Kayenta"
by Harvey Leake (2018)

This final chapter in Sisters of the Sage *is dedicated to another "real life heroine" in Zane Grey's life. Louisa Wetherill was the wife of John Wetherill, the trader who accompanied Grey on several of his trips to Rainbow Bridge. As you will see in this article by Harvey Leake, Louisa was a courageous friend to the Navajo, Hopi and Piute people. Her knowledge of the Native American people played a huge role in shaping Zane Grey's novel* The Vanishing American *and indigenous people in general. The Wetherills inspired several characters in Grey's works, with Louisa's role as Mrs. Withers being a true reflection of the trader's wife.*

Zane Grey

THE NAVAJOS ARE JUST LIKE OTHER FOLKS,"

Slim Woman said to Clyde Kluckhohn, a budding anthropologist. Slim Woman was the name given by the Navajos to Louisa Wade Wetherill of Kayenta, Arizona—my great grandmother. She lived with the People for decades, admired them dearly, and understood them deeply. She cautioned Kluckhohn that, because of the variations in human character from person to person, generalizations about any large group of people should be avoided. Kluckhohn was taken aback by her statement and found it difficult to accept. "That is better than 'the ignorant savage' of the worst element in the Indian service and better than 'the noble redman' of the worst sentimentalists; but still, I feel, the Navajos have a way of their own and a very special way," he argued. "I think perhaps one would get close to it if one said that the Navajo was like a charming but slightly spoiled child who had a strangely strong and powerful love of beauty which one doesn't usually associate with children." As the years went on, his point of view on this subject improved. In later life, he authored several books on the Navajos, including, with Dorothea Leighton, *The Navaho* and *Children of the People: The Navaho Individual and His Development*.

Kluckhohn was just one of many interesting people that Slim Woman influenced during her forty-five years among the Navajos. Folks came from far away to her home in Kayenta, Arizona, near Monument Valley, to gain understanding, seek advice, and see first-hand the qualities of a culture that was decidedly different from anything they had experienced theretofore. Louisa's husband, John Wetherill, was an authority on the archaeology of the region and likewise was often engaged in educating the guests on that subject and the wonders of the surrounding countryside.

One of the attractions of Kayenta in the early days was its remoteness and difficulty of access. Visitors felt that they were traveling into the past when they made the long, rough journey to the Wetherill's' doorway. "Kayenta is a gateway, like Thibet, to the Unknown. It is a frontier, perhaps the last real frontier in the States. Only Piutes and Navajos brave the stupendous Beyond," wrote Winifred Hawkridge Dixon, an early adventurer.

Since the time of Columbus, non-Indians have struggled to comprehend the enigmatic Indian world view, which is so different than the familiar one brought across the Atlantic by recent immigrants. Interpretations ranged the gamut from hatred and the desire to kill the "ignorant savages" to phony emulation of the "noble redman" by Indian wannabes. But the prevalent approach settled into a general consensus that the Indians, while fully human, are somehow lacking in their abilities to quickly adapt to the superior ways of modern society, and that they need to be helped along that pathway. Rare are those who dare to suggest that there is something of value to be learned from traditional Native Americans, and that modern people might be the ones who are in need of change.

Louisa Wetherill's most famous student was Theodore Roosevelt who, with his sons Archibald and Quentin and cousin Nicholas, lingered a few days at the Wetherill home before and after their pack trip to the Rainbow Natural Bridge. This was in August, 1913, several years after the end of Roosevelt's tenure as president and shortly after he lost his bid for reelection under the Bull Moose Party. He was interested in seeing Louisa's reproductions of Navajo sand paintings and hearing her ideas about relations between Indians and non-Indians. She wrote out for him two Navajo prayers she had recorded— "Prayer to the Dawn" and "Prayer to the Big Black Bear."

Theodore Roosevelt at Kayenta, Arizona, August 1913

Unfortunately, Roosevelt no longer had much influence on the public arena, so the lessons that Slim Woman shared with him had less of an outlet for bettering public opinion or government policy than would have been the case if he had still been President. However, he did pass on his insights to the readers of his 1916 book, *A Book-Lover's Holidays in the Open*. Of Slim Woman, he wrote:

Mrs. Wetherill was not only versed in archeological lore concerning ruins and the like, she was also versed in the yet stranger and more interesting archology of the Indian's own mind and soul.... If Mrs. Wetherill could be persuaded to write on the mythology of the Navajos, and also on their present-day psychology—by which somewhat magniloquent term I mean their present ways and habits of thought—she would render an invaluable service. She not only knows their language; she knows their minds; she has the keenest sympathy not only with their bodily needs, but with their mental and spiritual processes; and she is not in the least afraid of them or sentimental about them when they do wrong. They trust her so fully that they will speak to her without reserve about those intimate things of the soul which they will never even hint at if they suspect want of sympathy or fear ridicule.

The Kayenta region often served as a field school for university students who ventured there to learn first-hand about subjects such as archaeology, anthropology, and ethnology. Slim Woman served as an able interpreter of Navajo culture for the scholars, and she facilitated gaining them access to the homes and ceremonies of her Navajo friends. Professor Byron Cummings of the University of Utah regularly brought his archaeology students to Kayenta. One of them, Joseph F. Anderson, recorded his impressions of Slim Woman: "The person who seems to be influencing the life of Navajos most is Mrs. John Wetherill of the Kayenta trading post, Arizona. This cultured woman wields more power among them than any chief, or 'head man'. She is a white woman adopted into the tribe and is a real leader among them, holding her position as a recognition by the Indians of her sympathetic interest in their life. A queen could hardly be more loved by her subjects. She is at once the judge, physician, interpreter, adviser and best friend of her devoted wards."

Some of the college groups that came to Kayenta were from Ivy-League universities. Harvard students in particular had the reputation of being arrogant and condescending toward Westerners, and they had been taught that Native Americans reflected an earlier, primitive stage in humanity's ever-improving, evolutionary climb. They were sometimes surprised to discover appealing character traits among these "backward" folks that were novel to anything they had seen or learned back East.

One notable Harvard student was Oliver La Farge, who first came to Kayenta in 1921 to study Southwestern archaeology. His trip did not start out well. Upon reaching the trading post at Cameron, Arizona, on the southern border of the Navajo country, he was taken aback when three Navajos came into the store. "These men must be the real article, the savages of the hinterland," La Farge recounted in his book, *Raw Material*. "They wore ragged work clothes, two of them had battered hats, the third, a dark, dirty headband. I remember the contrast of the bright turquoise in their ears, but nothing else was picturesque about them, they were merely shabby and surprisingly dark. I had had an idea that Indians were a rather light, bronze colour.

These men seemed purple. I found their expressions expressionless and stupid."

The students traveled from there to Tsegi Canyon, a landscape that, by almost all accounts, is stunningly beautiful. La Farge found it otherwise, describing it as "a howling ash-heap". "Its mile-wide floor was arid, useless. Its cliffs were too aggressive, the spruce and fir up in the crannies were a cheat. The heat danced on the flat and echoed off the walls."

Their next destination was the Wetherill's' place, and the visit there was like a conversion experience for the young Oliver. "We had spent one night at Kayenta," he recalled. "No one could be even that short a time in the Wetherill's' house, hearing them talk, seeing the beautiful things hanging on their walls, without catching some of the riches to be found among the Navajos and being stimulated to some desire to learn for himself. These Indians in the northern part of the reservation were quite different from the ones I saw at Cameron. As a matter of fact, I've never seen those purple ones again, they seem to have appeared out of nowhere that first day, a different race, to disappear again forever."

The Wetherill house at Kayenta was like a museum.

Even the scenery looked different. "Our camp was on a sandy knoll in the shade of some Maxfield Parrish piñon trees under a Maxfield Parrish sky," La Farge wrote. "I began to see the country with a rush and to know that it was beautiful and that I loved it." He resolved to change his major from archaeology to ethnology and to focus his studies on the Navajos. "The Indians had got me," he proclaimed.

La Farge's later understanding of the cultural difference between non-Indians and Indians was more sensible than Kluckhohn's. "I can clear the decks here by stating that Indians are not idyllic, any more than I am. They are just as stupid and just as intelligent as we are, just as noble and just as mean, just as good and just as bad.... They are different from us, strong in some things where we are weak, weak where we are strong."

Oliver La Farge had many notable accomplishments in his later life, but the one he is best known for is his authorship of *Laughing Boy*, a novel about a young Navajo man. It was acclaimed as portraying Indians as real human beings and awarded the Pulitzer Prize in 1930. He acknowledged the Wetherills for their role in making the story a success.

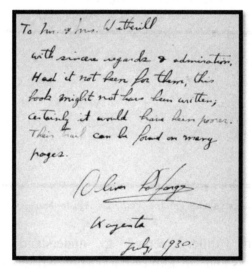

Oliver La Farge's inscription to the Wetherills in his presentation copy of Laughing Boy.

Of even greater consequence in the annals of Kayenta history was a 1923 visit by John Collier, an activist who had recently relocated from the East to California. He was making the rounds to educate himself on the Indian tribes of the Southwest and came to the Slim Woman's home to learn about the Navajos. She outlined some changes that were needed in government involvement with the Indians, and Collier was much impressed with her insights. "The ancient world and the American present meet in her personality as perhaps in no other personality alive," he wrote. "No one knows so well as she the simple yet enormous things possible for and with the Navajos."

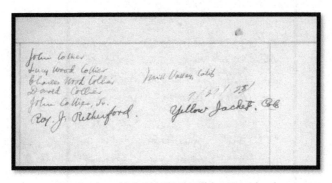

Guests signed into the Wetherills' register book.

John Collier seemed to understand the uniqueness and wisdom of the Navajo world view more profoundly than either Kluckhohn or La Farge. "They believe that a man's thought influences the cosmos; and that a venomous thought, or a hate or a fear, draws evil out of the hidden world, acting somehow like a magnet toward evil, and causes sickness and all ruin. Their discipline primarily is a search for joyous thought—for beauty and love; for these draw good from the hidden world, and are efficacious to produce good in the universe beyond man…. We have lost these realities; perhaps our race never knew them."

Slim Woman kept in touch with Collier and informed him of abuses that were taking place at the Bureau of Indian Affairs agency and boarding school in Tuba City, Arizona. Collier sent out letters of complaint, particularly against the Superintendent there, Chester L. Walker. Walker appealed to the Commissioner of Indian Affairs in Washington, asking if something could be done to stop the harassment. The Commissioner replied that Walker should ignore Collier, and eventually he would go away. He did not. In 1933 FDR appointed him as Commissioner of Indian Affairs, and Walker was promptly transferred to an agency in Montana where he lasted for just a short time.

In his role as Commissioner, Collier ended the decades-old government policy of cultural assimilation of Native Americans and implemented a New Deal for the Indians—self-determination. Gone was the forced attendance of Indian children at boarding schools and attempts to eradicate their traditional identities and beliefs. Collier's new policies reflected some of Slim Woman's ideas, such as establishment of local day schools, which enabled the children to gain an education while continuing to live with their families in familiar surroundings.

In later life, John Collier wrote a book about the Southwestern Indians he titled *On the Gleaming Way*. In it he expressed his sincere respect for the Navajo way of life and the inspiration that modern people could gain from learning about it. "So poor they are.... Yet the note which their life strikes is exuberance and joy, a singing note and the note of the dance and the dancing star.... How can so rich a flower bloom in a soil so rocky and nearly waterless? In terms of life, not of goods, it is we who are poor, not the Navajo."

Wolfkiller

Slim Woman authored her own book that set forth the best of the Navajo tradition—an oral history of a dear friend named Wolfkiller who told her about the wise lessons he had been taught by his grandfather and mother when he was just a boy— the "path of light". "All things are beautiful and full of interest if you observe them closely and study them," the grandfather said. "Keep your thoughts on the beautiful things you see around you. They may not seem beautiful to you at first, but if you look at them carefully you will soon learn that everything has some beauty in it."

Sadly, a publisher rejected Slim Woman's attempts to get the book into print when she completed it in the early 1930s. They thought that it was fictional and said it would be of no interest to modern readers. The manuscript languished in the family archives for seventy-five years until its value was finally recognized and it was made available as the book, *Wolfkiller: Wisdom from a Nineteenth-Century Navajo Shepherd*. In it, Slim Woman's passion for sharing the deep insights of her Navajo friends is clearly revealed. It is impossible to fully grasp the full extent of her legacy, because she influenced so many people and they, undoubtedly, used her ideas to influence many others.

HARVEY LEAKE began researching the history of his pioneering ancestors, the Wetherills of the Four Corners region, more than thirty years ago. His investigations have taken him to libraries, archives, and the homes of family elders whose recollections, photographs, and memorabilia have brought the story to life. His field research has led him to remote trading post sites in the Navajo country and some of the routes used by his great-grandfather, John Wetherill, to access the intricate canyon country of the Colorado Plateau. Harvey was born and raised in Prescott, Arizona. He is a semi-retired electrical engineer

Zane Grey

Three muses sitting on a rock on the Colorado River in the Grand Canyon. They are (L-R) Lillian Wilhelm, Dorothy Ackerman and Mildred Smith. Both Dorothy and Mildred joined Zane after 1915-1916. (L. Tom Perry Collection, BYU, MSS8710, Box 84)

APPENDIX A

ZANE GREY'S MUSES

Some fans of Zane Grey's works use an almost mythical term for his "literary assistants "and "secretaries." They refer to the young entourage of women, often in their teens, as "Zane Grey's Muses." This nickname seems appropriate since Grey told his wife, Dolly, that they were inspirations for the heroines in his novels much like the muses of Greek poetry.

The images provided here show six of not less than twelve of Grey's young muses. These young women provided services to Zane Grey for various periods of time from 1912 to 1929. Included are images of Lillian Wilhelm, Claire Wilhelm, Dorothy Ackerman, Louise Anderson, Elma Schwarz and Mildred Smith. Their inclusion here perhaps will give you an idea of how the author envisioned many of the heroines in the *Women Westward*.

Lillian Wilhelm was Dolly Grey's cousin. She is shown here in
native regalia loaned her by Louisa Wetherill for a party in
Kayenta, AZ. Lillian traveled extensively with Zane Grey as well as
illustrating some early novels and decorating his homes. (Courtesy
of the John and Louisa Wetherill Collection)

Louise Anderson was a teenager who lived with Zane Grey in his Catalina Island Pueblo from 1921 to 1923 to "study literature under the direction of the noted author." (L. Tom Perry Collections, BYU, MSS 8710, Box 48)

Elma Schwarz (left) is another of Dolly Grey's cousins who was involved with Grey from at least 1912 to 1921. Lillian Wilhelm is seated to the right. Photo taken in 1912 in Lackawaxen, PA. (L. Tom Perry Collection, BYU, MSS 8710, Box 48)

Zane Grey

*Lillian Wilhelm on roof, Elma Schwarz and John Wetherill (right) at
Betatakin Cliff Dwelling, now in Navajo National Monument (John
and Louisa Wetherill Collection)*

*Lillian Wilhelm, Elma Schwartz and Lillian's younger sister, Claire,
in Long Key, FL ca 1916. Claire traveled with Grey until 1921 when
she left him to be married.
(L. Tom Perry Collections, BYU, MSS 8277, Box 1)*

Ladies mounted on 1917 Grand Canyon trip with Grey. (L. Tom Perry Collection, BYU, MSS8710, Box 84)

Zane Grey and Mildred Smith riding during same trip to the Grand Canyon (L. Tom Perry Collection, BYU, MSS8710, Box 74)

Dorothy Ackerman, Claire Wilhelm, Mildred Smith and Grey's sister-in-law, Reba Grey, during 1917 trip to Flattop Mountain in Colorado. (L. Tom Perry Collection, BYU, MSS P-85, Box 1)

Dorothy Ackerman, Clair Wilhelm on wagon, likely outside Kayenta, AZ (L. Tom Perry Collection, BYU, MSS 8277, Box 1)

Sisters of the Sage

APPENDIX B: COPYRIGHTS

"Betty Zane"
Betty Zane © 1903 Charles Francis Press

"Lucinda Huett"
30,000 on the Hoof © 1940 Zane Grey, Inc.

Milly Fayre"
The Thundering Herd © 1925 Zane Grey

"Lucy Watson"
Under the Tonto Rim © 1926 Zane Grey

"Lenore Anderson"
The Desert of Wheat ©1919 Harper and Brothers

"Edith Watrous"
"Outlaws of Palouse" © 1934 Zane Grey, Inc.

"Majesty Hammond"
The Light of the Western Stars © 1914 Harper & Brothers

"Nell Wells"
The Spirit of the Border © 1906 A.L. Burt Co.

"Jane Withersteen"
Riders of the Purple Sage © 1912 Zane Grey

"Marian Warner"
The Vanishing American © 1925 Zane Grey

"Dolly Grey"
Previously Unpublished © 1917 Dolly Grey

"Louisa Wetherill"
"Slim Woman of Kayenta" ©2018 Harvey Leake

Sisters of the Sage

APPENDIX C:
REFERENCES

Donahue, John, *Who's Who in the Western Fiction of Zane Grey* (2008) McFarland and Company

Kant, Candace C., *Dolly and Zane Grey: Letters from a Marriage* (2008) University of Nevada Press

Pauly, Thomas H., *Zane Grey: His Life, His Adventures, His Women* (2007) University of Illinois Press

Pfeiffer, Charles G., *Zane Grey: A Study in Values-Above and Beyond the West* (2005) Zane Grey's West Society

Wheeler, Joseph L. (compiler), *Zane Grey Master Character Index* (2017) Zane Grey's West Society

New Zane Grey Collector, Zane Grey's West, Zane Grey Review, Zane Grey Reporter, Zane Grey Quarterly, Zane Grey Explorer- Newsletters of Zane Grey's West Society from 1984 to Present

ZANE GREY'S WEST SOCIETY

Zane Grey's West Society is the world's pre-eminent non-profit organization dedicated to preserving and sharing the history and works of the great Western Romance author, Zane Grey.

We welcome new members at zgws.org or www.facebook.com/ZaneGreysWestSociety

G.M F

© 1968 g. m. farley

Made in the USA
Middletown, DE
23 August 2023

37235544R00205